THE BAYOU BULLETIN

Explosive Beginning to Delacroix-Weston Marriage!

The fairy-tale wedding reception for Joanna Delacroix Gideon and Logan Weston was marred by a bomb blast on the grounds of Riverwood estate last week. Champagne was flowing freely and guests were marveling at the perfect weather when a wedding gift exploded as it was being carried into the house. Charlotte Delacroix, youngest of Judge Justin Delacroix's daughters, as well as a member of the catering staff, sustained minor injuries in the blast.

Guests were particularly concerned about the victims of the explosion because Charly, as she is known to all, a rookie police officer, had been on the force for only four days when she was seriously injured in a shooting incident at Swampy's Bar and Grill. She has been recuperating at home, and there has been widespread speculation that the recent explosion might be related in some way to the shooting at Swampy's, which claimed the life of Charly Delacroix's partner, Officer Frank Weatherspoon, a twelve-year veteran of the force.

It is a certainty that the entire Delacroix clan would never have imagined that the celebration of a joyous event could turn tragic. Guests left quickly after the explosion. The mood of the wedding became subdued, as the injured needed attending....

Kelsey Roberts is acknowledged
as the author of this work.

ISBN 0-373-82568-4

SOMEONE TO WATCH OVER HER

DELTA JUSTICE

Someone to Watch Over Her

KELSEY ROBERTS

Harlequin Books

TORONTO • NEW YORK • LONDON
AMSTERDAM • PARIS • SYDNEY • HAMBURG
STOCKHOLM • ATHENS • TOKYO • MILAN
MADRID • WARSAW • BUDAPEST • AUCKLAND

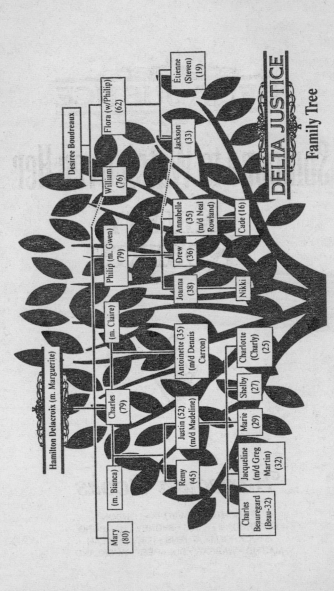

DELTA JUSTICE
Family Tree

Hamilton Delacroix (m. Marguerite)

Mary (80)

Charles (79)

(m. Bianca)

(m. Claire)

Philip (m. Gwen) (79)

Desiree Boudreaux

William (76)

Flora (w/Philip) (62)

Étienne (Steven) (19)

Jackson (33)

Remy (45)

Justin (52) (m/d Madeline)

Antoinette (35) (m/d Dennis Carron)

Joanna (38)

Drew (36)

Annabelle (35) (m/d Neal Rowland)

Cade (16)

Nikki

Jacqueline (m/d Greg Martin) (32)

Marie (29)

Shelby (27)

Charlotte (Charly) (25)

Charles Beauregard (Beau-32)

CAST OF CHARACTERS

Charly Delacroix—the youngest of Justin Delacroix's daughters, a police officer wounded in the line of duty, and determined to get to the bottom of a shooting that makes no sense.

Marshall Avery—personal trainer, hired by Justin to watch over his daughter Charly. Avery has an agenda all his own, and the smarts and charisma to take on the most prickly client he's ever had!

Beau Delacroix—Charly's big brother. He gives new meaning to the term *overprotective*. Especially where his sister and Marshall Avery are concerned.

Police Chief Harrington—Charly's boss. He's convinced she doesn't have what it takes to make the grade. Charly is determined to prove him wrong.

Jada Crowley—Charly's good friend. An ugly incident in her past is threatening her future. And Charly doesn't take kindly to threats to her friends.

Rico Tesconti—a crime boss Charly suspects in connection with the shooting of her partner. Or is he after Charly?

Dear Reader,

I was very happy when I was assigned Charly's story in the DELTA JUSTICE series. My brain immediately began listing the similarities between this character and myself. I'm the youngest child in a family that rarely lacks for opinions—so is Charly. I come from a family that considers anything less than perfection failure—so does Charly. I'm a junk food addict—so I made Charly one. Okay, so that's where the similarities end, but it was a great way to start a project.

Charly is a patrol officer, and that necessitated a little research. I am lucky to have a friend who is a police lieutenant and was willing to take me out on patrol with him. So, on a very cold January night I ventured out with Lieutenant Chuck Mounts. I learned a lot, but mostly I learned that the last time I stayed out all night I was probably twenty-two and it was a whole lot easier back then!

Marshall Avery is my favorite kind of hero. There's nothing more intriguing to write about than a man with a secret, and Marshall has a big one. He's also a little autocratic, which doesn't set too well with independent Charly. It was fun to take these two people and put them in positions where they had to depend on one another.

Both Charly and Marshall discover that love isn't about the loss of identity or autonomy. With real love, the kind that lasts a lifetime, you gain the things that really matter—a partner, a lover and a friend.

Happy reading.

Warmest regards,

Kelsey Roberts

PROLOGUE

HIS EYELASHES DIDN'T SO much as flutter as he captured the man in his sights. But then, this was his specialty. He felt his lips curl. What would his useless old man have thought if he could see him now? The old drunk had often told him—between vicious beatings—that he'd never be good at anything.

His line of vision was blocked for an instant by the red-and-blue strobe lights on top of the cruiser. The instant it was clear, he squeezed the trigger.

One down.

Slowly, he swung the rifle until he found his next target. The woman was getting out of the car, no doubt still trying to figure out what had happened to her partner. Adrenaline surged through him as he got her in the crosshairs. His full attention on the task at hand. The task that would put fifteen big ones in his account.

The scope allowed him a quick study of her profile from a safe distance of a hundred yards. Thanks to his custom-made silencer, she would never know what hit her. But he would.

"Damn," he muttered as she bolted around the squad car. He should have taken the shot when it was clear. No matter. Slowly, keeping the rifle trained in her direction, he squeezed the trigger. There was no sound, just the jerk of the barrel as the bullet soared toward its target.

"Clean," he whispered with a satisfied smirk when the woman spun from the force of the impact.

For a split second, he thought her eyes had found him. *Stupid.* There was no way the broad could see him in the dense pine underbrush. It didn't matter, anyway, he told himself as he began disassembling the gun with swift, masterful precision. He placed the weapon in his nylon bag, closed the bag and hoisted it onto his shoulder, stopping only long enough to collect the spent cartridges.

It wouldn't matter at all. She was dead.

CHAPTER ONE

"I'M IN LOVE."

"So is every other woman here." Ada Jane Crowley took a compact from her purse and checked her lipstick.

It was perfect, but Charly didn't bother telling her friend. She knew that Jada primped as often as she breathed. Primping was as much a part of the willowy blond as her tailored blazers and vast collection of hair accessories.

Beneath a clear Louisiana sky, the gardens of Riverwood, Charly's family home, had been decked out with fine crystal and silver on white-linen-covered tables, and enough flowers to cover a Rose Bowl float. But Charly paid no attention to her elegant surroundings, not to the glamorous guests—members of Louisiana's political and social elite who had come to help celebrate her cousin's Joanna's wedding. It was the view at the makeshift bar that she found compelling. And the object of her attention was oblivious to the fact that she was staring at him. She could look her fill and he didn't have a clue. It was perfect.

Perfection. That was the only way to describe six feet three inches of dark, brooding masculinity. He was even more ruggedly handsome than the guy on the billboard across from her apartment house. If only the Stetson wasn't shading his eyes. She guessed they'd be blue, cobalt blue. No, maybe green, like shimmering water.

Charly's breath caught when he pushed the hat back on his forehead and their eyes met. They weren't blue or green, but she'd been close with the water theme. They were black and hard, like a shark's.

"Oh, God!" Charly groaned, and quickly dropped her gaze. "He caught me ogling him. What should I do?"

Jada grinned. "You'll have to go into the house and slit your wrists."

"Thanks for the tip." She lifted a beer to her lips and took a long swallow just as the DJ played a Clint Black tune. "I think I've been out of circulation too long."

"*I* think you've finally realized that the good Lord put two sexes on this earth."

"You aren't helping," Charly breathed. "Is he still looking at me?"

"Yep."

She watched as Jada looked in the direction of the bar and smiled.

"Why did you do that?" Charly asked.

"To see if he was looking at you or me."

"And?"

"I'm surprised you can't feel the sizzle on your back. Lucky you. That one seems determined."

"What am I going to do?" Charly whispered, panicked. "He'll think I was—"

"Chill out, Charly," Jada admonished. "He's got to

be used to women looking at him. Hell's bells, any man who looks that fine probably only notices the women who *don't* look." Jada lifted the straw out of her glass and took a sip. It was a simple act, but it still conveyed femininity, something Charly felt she lacked completely. "Why don't you go talk to him?"

"Talk? To him?"

Jada's big blue eyes sparkled. "Yes, Charly. You just go up to him and introduce yourself."

"To a total stranger?"

"Once you introduce yourself, you won't be strangers. Besides, I don't know why you're so reluctant. Last time I checked, I was your only female friend. You know how to talk to men."

"Men *friends,*" Charly emphasized.

Jada's smile was slow and wicked. "I don't think he's the kind of man you go to for friendship."

"You'll burn in hell for those thoughts," Charly said with a small grin.

"What a way to go."

Charly groaned as she slid her feet out of the uncomfortable leather flats and let her toes play in the springy grass. "How much longer do you think we have to stay? I mean, Joanna and Logan are already married."

"Until you go talk to him. If you're worried about me, I can find a way home. Maybe Joanna and Logan will let me ride with them."

Charly sent her friend a sidelong glance. "I think the bride and groom have other plans." She toyed with the strand of pearls her sister Jax had insisted she wear with The Dress—the one and only dress she owned. "I'm ready to go. I feel silly like this."

"You look cute."

Charly hid her wince behind her hand. Cute—as in puppy, kitten, baby. She'd worn that adjective like a brand all her life. Now, in spite of the fact that she was twenty-five and a police officer, she was still cute.

"I look like a transvestite in this makeup." She grimaced as she used the linen napkin to wipe the remnants of the waxy lipstick off her mouth. "I can't stand wearing this dress..."

"You could have bought a new one, you know," Jada teased. "Most women do have more than one."

"Don't you start in on me, too," Charly pleaded softly. She squirmed and tugged at her hem. "I don't know how you stand dressing for success day in and day out. Owning only one dress saves me from the dreaded, time-consuming ritual of trying to choose the perfect outfit."

"I don't know how I do it, either," Jada admitted. "You look nice, Charly. Stop fidgeting."

"I really want to leave. Joanna and Logan won't notice. They're...besotted."

Joanna's laugh was lilting and feminine. It reminded Charly of her sisters. Marie, Jax and Shelby were all the feminine type, as well. Charly knew she was more like her older brother, Beau. Right down to her preference for masculine attire.

"So is your secret admirer. Do you know who he is?" Jada asked.

"Never seen him," Charly answered. "He's probably a friend of Logan's. Maybe he's a relative and he isn't admiring me.''

"Wanna bet? I wonder if he's married." Jada's voice trailed off dreamily.

"Go ask," Charly suggested. "He's probably dying to meet you."

Jada looked ready to burst. "Think again. He hasn't stopped looking at you for the last ten minutes. I think you should be the one to give him the third degree. It makes sense—you've got the investigative training."

"I don't need to talk to him."

Jada's eyes sparkled in the midday sun. "Really? Then please, share your brilliant powers of observation with me."

Charly turned in the direction of the man in question. Ignoring his pointed stare, she regarded him for less than a minute.

"Oh, great investigator," Jada whispered, "tell me about our urban cowboy."

"Not urban," Charly said. "His jeans have slack."

"Slack?"

"Real cowboys have slack in their pant legs when they're standing."

"Why?"

Charly grinned. "Because they want their jeans to be the right length when they're in the saddle. His boots are scuffed and worn, working-class, not department store issue. But something isn't right about him."

Jada sighed. "Could have fooled me."

"That shirt is custom made, and he probably only wears it for formal occasions."

"Do real cowboys come to weddings without their cowgirls?" Jada wanted to know.

Charly shrugged and let out a muffled curse as a sharp pain traveled down her right side. "I'm tired of sitting here listening to toasts and tittering. I'm going to walk. Want to come?"

"I like the view here," Jada sighed. "Besides, I don't want to miss the cake. If you're going, anyway, would you get my gift out of your car?"

"Sure." Charly grabbed her keys.

She made a quick survey of the area, then, finding no trace of her father, she scooped up her shoes and headed toward the house. Delacroix family functions could tax the patience of a saint.

Caterers and formally dressed servers were everywhere. Charly had to smile. Her grandfather Charles had spared no expense—despite the fact that this was his niece Joanna's second wedding. There were string quartets and rivers of champagne and the best seafood Louisiana had to offer. She grabbed a pastry filled with crab something or other from a silver tray as she passed through the garden doors. The house was only slightly cooler, probably because so many people were bustling about.

It really should have been her great-uncle Philip who was hosting this wedding. He *was* Joanna's father, after all. But their relationship had been strained ever since Joanna had left Philip's law firm to work for Charles Delacroix, instead. And the long-standing rift between the twin brothers had only made the situation pricklier.

Charly wouldn't have been surprised if Philip had pulled a no-show. But he had come. It wouldn't have been a good political move for the state senator to miss his own daughter's wedding, she thought cynically.

Charly headed out to the front porch. The lawn was a sea of cars. Waving off the valet attendant, she bounded down the steps toward her sporty convertible.

She took deep breaths as she went, savoring air that wasn't heavy with perfume and cigar smoke. Nothing would have made her happier than to jump in her car and drive until this restlessness she felt no longer gnawed at her gut. She hated weddings almost as much as she hated being dependent on her family.

The neatly wrapped gift was on the driver's seat. A second present had fallen to the floor. It must be part of Jada's gift, too. She leaned into the car to reach the package on the floor when the hair at the back of her neck suddenly stood on edge.

Turning and straightening in one smooth movement, she had her keys defensively positioned in her fist.

"You're fast," he said, smiling down at her.

It wasn't just a smile, though. It was a lethal weapon that rendered Charly mute.

He didn't try to come closer. In fact, he took such a relaxed, casual stance that she felt like a complete jerk for overreacting.

"I'm Marshall Avery." He didn't offer his hand. He made no attempt to make contact with her whatsoever.

Her brain switched to send out warning signals of a new kind. This cowboy had managed to electrify her entire being with a mere smile.

"If I offer to buy you a drink, will you tell me your name?"

"The drinks are free," she countered.

"I'll leave a garish tip, then."

He's flirting with me. Then her mind cleared. She suspected she knew what he was really after. Not wanting to see the joy in those midnight eyes, she turned back to the car and made a production of gathering the presents. "Her name is Jada Crowley and she works—"

Her voice vanished when she felt him come up behind her. It wasn't every day that she had powerful thighs pressed against her. The scent of woodsy cologne with an undertone of soap filled the air between them. Panic surged through her when his arm came around her. She felt the roughness of denim and the butter softness of his cotton shirt. But most of all, she felt his heat.

"Let me," he whispered.

"I will not—" Charly never finished the sharp rebuke. Not once she realized what he intended to do. Hating the blush she could feel on her warm cheeks, she held her breath as he slowly reached around her for the presents.

When he straightened and stood back from her, Charly wasn't at all sure she was happy to lose the feel of his warm body. This was sheer idiocy. Too much sun and too much beer, she insisted, though she hadn't even finished the bottle. "Thanks," she murmured without looking up. "If you want me to introduce you to Jada, I will."

His squared fingertips brushed her arm, giving life to every cell of her being in the process. "Who is Jada?"

Charly looked at him then. He was all chiseled angles and perfect teeth. His hat was pushed up on his forehead, and she could easily see the thick, inky lashes that should have been too feminine but weren't. He shifted the packages beneath one muscular arm and his head dipped to one side. "Jada?"

Charly blinked and forced a small smile. "She's the woman I was sitting with. The one who looks like Malibu Barbie. But she's no airhead," Charly warned.

His laughter was rich and deep, a velvety caress to her ears. "I'll have to take your word for it. Why do you think I want to meet Barbie?"

"Jada," Charly corrected him as she nervously shifted her shoes from one hand to the other.

"Jada?" he repeated.

"Every man with a pulse wants to meet Jada," Charly answered. *Why do I have to meet a man like this when I'm barefoot?*

"I'm not every man."

"No joke."

"Was that a compliment?"

"No." She looked up into those dark, mesmerizing pools. His body looked hard as granite, softened only by that killer smile. But there was more to this smiling cowboy. "It was merely an observation. I should get back."

"You put up your shields faster than the Starship Enterprise," he said as he fell in beside her.

"And if you value your dilithium crystals, you'll stop bothering me."

He grabbed her hand and held it, stopping her progress along with her ability to breathe normally. It would have been undignified to snatch her hand away, so she settled for giving him her most poisonous glare.

The playful gleam in his eyes wasn't the reaction she had hoped for. "You don't mince words, do you, darlin'?"

"My name isn't darlin'," she said. If only she was more like her sisters. Marie would freeze him with her aloofness. Jax would just stare at him with cool confidence. Shelby would threaten to file suit. Charly didn't have a weapon, at least not one that would work against that sexy smile and those smoky eyes.

"I'm just making do until you tell me your name," he reasoned. Slowly, he lifted her hand to his lips and brushed a kiss across her knuckles that quickened her pulse. The warmth of his breath and the softness of his lips sent her mind racing into all sorts of uncharted territories.

"Charly."

He released her hand immediately. "Nice to meet you, Charly."

"Why did you do that?"

He winked. "I wanted to."

"Do you always do what you want?"

"Always," he drawled.

The single word caused a flutter in her belly. *Defenses up—don't look into his eyes!* "Well, Marshall Avery, I don't know what your game is, but—"

"This isn't a game."

"Fine," she said, raking her fingers through her hair. "I don't know what your scam is, but—"

"Are you always so suspicious? You aren't old enough to be so cynical."

Charly regarded him for a minute before focusing on the turquoise nugget on the clasp of his bolero tie. "I'm old enough and cynical enough to know a phony when I see one."

"That's a little harsh."

"You might look like some harmless cowboy, but you really should have picked a more realistic part to play."

"Part?"

Charly slipped her shoes back on. "The clothes are right. It's the accessories that snagged you."

"Accessories?"

"A real cowboy doesn't wear a Rolex or have his ear pierced. Now, if you'll excuse me."

She walked away, trying her best to infuse some arrogance in her step. It would have been a bit easier if she hadn't been wearing such tight, uncomfortable shoes that scrunched her toes. It would have been a lot easier if she hadn't been absolutely certain he was watching.

SHE DIDN'T HAVE A CLUE, he mused as he shifted her packages in his arm. She sure as hell wasn't the child he'd expected. Nope, and that thought brought a slow smile to his lips. The way she tilted her chin, the defiance in those beautiful gray eyes. And let's not forget that body, his memory prompted. How could he? The brief encounter by the car still had him slightly off balance. That shapeless black dress was hiding a very shapely form.

So she thought he would pass her over for her friend? That was pretty revealing. He supposed it made sense. The friend was a looker, in that polished, don't-touch-me-my-nails-are-wet kind of way.

Maybe this wouldn't be so bad, after all. He rubbed the long-healed scar on his earlobe. The lady hadn't missed a trick. He stored that in his growing file on Charly Delacroix, certain he could use it later—to his advantage. That was how the game was played.

Marshall straightened his hat as he climbed the porch steps.

"I'll take that, sir," a young woman said, relieving him of the presents.

Marshall grunted thanks, then made his way to the back garden. His keen eyes scanned the crowded lawn, and it didn't take long to find her. She was predictable. She was seated at the same table, locked in a private, whispered conversation with the Barbie doll. He stored that tidbit, as well.

"Have you met my daughter?" Justin Delacroix asked, emerging from the house to stand beside Marshall.

"Not formally," Marshall hedged.

"We can remedy that," the older man said as he motioned in Charly's direction with his hand.

Marshall shrugged. He would have liked to wait a bit longer, let her share every detail with her friend before being introduced. Justin seemed to have a different idea, and he was in no position to argue with the man.

Marshall followed Justin, his eyes still on Charly. Her features were fine-boned, delicate, and her skin had a natural glow, completely devoid of makeup. Her hair was raven black, glinting with blue highlights in the sunlight. It was cut in a practical bob, and that made him smile. She was so different from the other Delacroix women he had met. Her sisters all had long hair and didn't shy away from enhancing their natural beauty with cosmetics. Charly was definitely an individual. Had circumstances been different, he might have tried to discover why she was so determined to hide her femininity.

A white ball sailed away from a group of boys playing off to one side of the reception area and headed in Charly's direction. She reached out her hand and snagged it like a major-leaguer, probably saving the kids from a major tongue-lashing for playing baseball so close to the guests. Her return throw was equally impressive and inspired giggles and applause from the boys.

Although Marshall admired her throw, Justin certainly didn't.

"Charly, can't you behave like a lady for one afternoon?"

Marshall watched the smile fade from her face. She turned to look at her father, and when her eyes caught sight of Marshall her expression chilled.

"Yes, Daddy." She got up on tiptoe to place a kiss on her father's cheek.

Justin chuckled and wrapped his arm around her shoulder. Despite his earlier criticism, Marshall recognized male pride when he saw it. Justin was definitely proud of his youngest. "This is not the time to be playing ball."

"I know." Charly ran a hand along her father's lapel. "It won't happen again."

"And put your shoes back on," Justin admonished. "This is hardly a picnic."

"Yes, Daddy," Charly returned automatically, regretting having slipped off her shoes once again. "Can you talk them into cutting the cake? I want to get Jada back to town before too long."

"Jada," Justin said as he took the willowy blonde's outstretched hand. "You're looking lovely as ever."

"And you're as handsome as ever, Justin," Jada purred. "I was just asking Charly about you."

"Telling my secrets, Charly?"

"Jada's knows *all* your secrets, Daddy," Charly teased. "She's known you for twenty years and she still wants to marry you."

Justin winked at Charly's friend. "You know my heart is yours, Jada. I just don't want to have to stand in that long line of suitors you have."

Jada placed her hand against her forehead with dramatic flair. "I'd send them all away for you."

"Enough," Justin said, laughing. "I'm too old to do justice to a woman like you, Ada Jane." He turned to Marshall. "But I do have someone I'd like you lovely ladies to meet."

Marshall struggled to keep his expression bland, though his eyes were riveted to Charly's.

"This is Marshall Avery."

"We met in the parking lot," Charly said. "I don't know what he's told you, but—"

Justin silenced the strong-willed daughter with a mere inclination of his head.

"*We* didn't," Jada said, offering her hand. "I'm Jada Crowley."

Marshall politely closed his fingers over her heavily jeweled hand. "Miss Crowley."

"Jada's family are old family friends of ours. Jada works in the family business with her father...investment banking."

"Jada's a vice president," Charly added. "She handles overseas acquisitions."

Justin studied his daughter closely for a moment, perhaps even critically, Marshall thought. "The important thing is she did right by her family," Justin said.

Judging by the subtle fury in Charly's gray eyes, Marshall guessed Justin had scored a direct hit. Charly looked as if smoke might come pouring out of her ears at any moment.

"What do you do, Mr. Avery?" Jada asked to cover the awkward silence.

"Yes," Charly breathed sweetly. "What is it you do?"

"Whatever I want," Marshall answered smoothly, his eyes biting into Charly. "I thought we'd already discussed that."

"What?" Justin asked, looking puzzled.

"Nothing," Charly answered.

"I've hired Mr. Avery," Justin announced.

"A cowboy lawyer?" Charly scoffed.

"I hired him for you," her father said.

Marshall knew it wouldn't be a good idea to give in to his laughter. Oh, but he wanted to. The look on her face was priceless.

"For me? I don't need a lawyer, daddy."

"He's not a lawyer, Charly. He's a personal trainer. Mr. Avery has agreed to whip you back into shape."

Marshall waited for the explosion. When it came, it was unexpected. Charly didn't explode. One of the packages he'd carried for her just moments earlier did.

CHAPTER TWO

"I'M FINE," Charly insisted.

"Make use of those muscles, Marshall," Justin instructed. "Carry her into the parlor. She can rest on the sofa until we get Lucas to have a look at her and see if she sustained any injuries in the blast."

Charly tried to free herself from Marshall's arms. He was carrying her as if she weighed no more than a sack of potatoes.

"This isn't necessary," she grumbled.

"But it sure is fun," he replied, giving her a little squeeze.

Humiliated, Charly closed her eyes, hoping this was yet another of her bad dreams. She refused to believe that she was actually being held against his solid body. "If you're in the mood to play Boy Scout, you could go back outside to help."

"I've been a lot of things, but Boy Scout was never one of them."

"Put her down there," Justin directed. "Odelle! Bring in some bandages and some antiseptic!"

Charly was lowered onto the soft cushions so gently that she almost didn't listen to what her father was saying. When his words finally registered, she started to rise. "I'm fine, Daddy."

"You'll stay there until we have a chance to have you seen to."

Marshall sat on the edge of the sofa, his stern expression daring her to move. Charly wasn't sure which one of the men she should kill first. "It's just a scratch," she insisted.

"I'll have a look."

She glared at Marshall. "Touch me and die."

"Don't be difficult, Charly," Justin said. "The paramedics said we should clean those abrasions."

"Which is exactly what I intend to do. And you, Daddy, should be outside helping Grandfather calm the guests. It's not every wedding that has a bomb go off at it. And let me know how that woman from the catering service is doing." With athletic grace, Charly managed to swing her legs around Marshall's formidable size and get to her feet. "I'm going to take a shower now," she told the two men. "And I haven't required help bathing since I was six."

"Your daughter sure is prickly," she heard Marshall say as she made her escape.

Taking the steps two at a time, Charly went to her assigned room in the west wing of the house. She had purposefully asked for one of the guest rooms when she'd had to move back home after being injured on the job almost eight months earlier. Returning to her old bedroom would have been a little too much like turning back the clock on her hard-won independence. Maybe she should have taken over Jax's cabin, now that her older sister was in her new home with her husband and two stepchildren.

She headed into the bathroom and glanced in the

full-length mirror. When she saw the purple bruise forming on her shoulder, she winced. "Yuck." Of course it had to be the shoulder she'd already injured. Carefully, she peeled The Dress down until it pooled at her ankles. She wasn't sure if it would survive a dry cleaning. Unidentifiable debris was sprinkled in her hair, and mud smudged her face.

The mud didn't bother her. The new injury to her shoulder did. "Damn it!" she seethed as she tried to raise her right arm. The pain and stiffness were back with a vengeance. All those months of rest down the tubes.

As she started the bathwater, she realized she was being selfish and self-centered. One of the employees of the catering service had been injured in the blast. The woman had suffered burns when the gifts had exploded just a few feet from where she'd been doing nothing more dangerous than serving pâté.

When the bathtub was filled, Charly stripped out of her remaining clothes and submerged herself in the warm water up to her chin. The bruise ached and her skin burned where it had been scraped by bits of flying debris. Closing her eyes, she tried not to think back to the other time she'd felt like this, but she just couldn't help it...

"I SURE DON'T SEE any signs of a B and E," Frank Weatherspoon *said as he brought the unit to a halt in front of Swampy's Bar and Grill.* "I don't see why anyone'd bother to break into this hole. Everyone knows Hank cleans out the register when he closes up."

Charly laughed as she adjusted her hat. "He gave me the creeps when we were here the other night," she said. "How is it that you know him, anyway?"

Frank shrugged. "I've lived around these parts all my life. Hank and I go way back."

"And?" Charly prompted.

Frank reached down to open the snap on his holster. "What?"

"You sounded sad just then. Is there something more about Hank that you're not telling me?"

"Come on, Delacroix. Save your probing questions for the interrogation room."

Adrenaline pumped in her veins. She felt invincible. Not because of the gun on her belt or the rifle in the trunk. No, this rush was from knowing she had finally achieved her dream. She wasn't little Charly anymore, she was now Officer Delacroix.

"We'd best take a look," Frank said. "Not that we'll find anything more than a few health department violations."

"I'm ready." Charly had enough enthusiasm for both of them. Apparently, it wasn't lost on her partner.

"This is just one of thousands of dead calls you'll get during your career. For some sick reason, people get their jollies calling 911." Frank opened his door and got out. "In a few months you'll be as jaded as I am."

"Impossible," Charly said as she checked and rechecked her utility belt. "When I hit the twelve-year mark, I'll still want to catch the bad guys."

"C'mon, Delacroix." Frank grinned. "Let's go see if there's anything worth arresting in this—"

Charly's head whipped up when she heard the whoosh of air. Then everything seemed to move in slow motion. She saw Frank's surprised look. His green eyes were wide as they changed colors along with the emergency lights. Dark blue, blue, purple. Dark blue, blue, purple. Then he was falling. His knees hit first. Then he just slumped backward.

"Frank!" Charly yelled as she scrambled out of the car. Her shoulder was hot. No, not her shoulder, her ear. No, not her ear, her head. Something spun her. Then it was dark...

CHARLY HURRIED OUT of the tub. Fear and frustration had her hands shaking. A few minutes later as she rubbed her hair with a towel, she tried to rid the fragmented memory of the shooting from her brain. It was getting worse. It used to only come to her in sleep. Almost eight months later and the memory of Frank's death haunted her waking hours, as well.

"I need to get back to work," she whispered. Wiping the condensation from the mirror, she regarded her reflection. "I'll be fine once I get back on the proverbial horse."

Only they wouldn't even let her in the stable. The Slidell Police Department had issued its verdict. She was welcome to her job *if* she made a full recovery. Translation: they would do anything to keep her from coming back. They thought she was responsible for Frank's death.

Maybe they were right. *If only I could remember...*

"So much for a full recovery," she grumbled as she tried—once more—to work her arm. The bullet had entered her shoulder, shattering the bone. The fragments of bone had caused the bullet to ricochet, allowing it to reenter just behind her right ear. "I hope I haven't done anything to the replacement," she muttered. The knowledge that she now had a plastic shoulder blade instead of bone was sort of creepy. "Bionic or not, I'm back to square one."

"You decent?" Marie called from the bedroom.

"Give me a sec!" Charly grabbed her robe and worked her sore arm into the sleeve.

She found her sister standing by the bed, wringing her hands. Marie Delacroix Henderson was a sight. Charly was always amazed at her sister's rather eclectic taste in accessories. Because of Joanna and Logan's wedding, Marie had toned down her style somewhat. There were only about two dozen bracelets on her arm, and her scarf was in muted shades of green. "Is that a dress, or are you wearing your sheets?"

Marie smiled. "I see getting blown up hasn't dulled your humor."

"I wasn't blown up, the gift table was." Charly went to the closet she hoped was only temporarily hers and grabbed her favorite jeans and a very large, very faded T-shirt.

She slipped back into the bathroom, leaving the door open a crack while Marie told her all about the aftermath of the explosion. The caterer had been the only person seriously injured, and the paramedics had assured the family that her injuries didn't seem to be life threatening.

"Joanna will certainly have some stories to tell her

grandchildren,'' Marie finished. She eyed Charly's outfit. "Shopping at the thrift store again?"

"Nope, I rolled a drunk for the shirt. The jeans date back to high school. So what have the police come up with?"

"I heard them say something about a cowboy," she began, "and I—"

"Tall, dark hair, dark eyes?" Charly asked.

Marie nodded. "I heard one of the detectives say they were going to talk to him."

"About what? Do they think Avery set the explosion? He's downstairs!" Charly cried. "We have to warn—"

"Calm down," Marie insisted. "First off, there's no one downstairs now except family. Second, who is Avery?"

"The cowboy from the wedding. He's some sort of personal trainer that Daddy hired."

"Oh, yes. Daddy introduced him to Lucas and me, but I'd forgotten his name. I'm sure he couldn't have anything to do with the explosion. The police aren't even sure what caused the blast." Marie came over and gave a lock of Charly's damp hair a tug. "The police are handling this. You have to concentrate on getting better."

"I am better. I want to know the direction of the investigation."

"All I know is that we're lucky no one was killed."

"Are there any suspects? Any—"

"Keep it up and I'll have Lucas sedate you."

"Speaking of tall, bland and medical, where is he?"

"Downstairs, waiting to provide you with the family discount on a house call."

"He's a pathologist," Charly said with feigned horror. "Is there something you haven't told me yet?"

"Sure," Marie answered, pretending grave seriousness. "You're still a brat."

"I'LL AGREE TO THAT at about the same time Odelle goes down to dance naked in the Quarter!"

Marshall tried to close the massive oak door as quietly as possible. Tossing his hat on a side table, he walked in the direction of the low, sultry voice and its contradictorily petite owner.

"My sister said the police wanted to talk to you. What happened? Didn't they have a jail cell available?" Charly demanded the instant he crossed the threshold.

"Nice to see you again, Miss Delacroix. Justin." He noted that Charly's father didn't appear to be in the best of moods. "Dr. Henderson, Mrs. Henderson."

"Everything squared away?" Justin asked.

"Kind of," Marshall answered as he joined the two men, who stood off to one side. Something told him there might be safety in numbers. "The locals are going to call in the FBI."

Charly's eyes were shimmering like the blade of a well-honed dagger. He met them in kind. "I take it your daughter isn't interested in what I have to offer?" he asked Justin.

Charly made a decidedly unladylike sound before she let loose with a string of expletives.

"Charlotte!" Justin barked sharply. "You know

how your grandfather feels about such language. You're a Delacroix.''

"And Beau isn't?" she shot back.

She might be small, but she sure didn't back off from a fight, Marshall mused.

"Beau is a man," Justin stated before he took a long swallow from the highball glass in his hand.

"And Beau's the one who taught me."

"Then your brother isn't a very *smart* man."

Marshall was truly amused, but he refused to let it show. Something told him Charly wouldn't appreciate being laughed at just now. "I've got my things out in the truck," he said after several minutes of strained silence had passed.

"Odelle will tell you where to put them."

"Don't bother Odelle," Charly said with a smile. "I'll be more than happy to tell Mr. Avery where he can put his things."

"I'll just bet you would." He smiled at the reckless glint in her eyes. "But I think I'll wait for your house-keeper."

"That won't be necessary," Charly said. "I'm not going to have my father throwing good money away on a personal trainer for me. We'll be happy to pay you for any inconvenience."

"He's staying," Justin announced. "And you'll mind your manners and treat him appropriately, as you were raised."

"You don't know how I was raised. You were never around," Charly snapped. There was a sudden, dead silence. "I'm so sorry, Daddy," she said, walking over to him and pressing herself against him.

Marshall didn't miss the pain that filtered into the older man's eyes. His opinion of Charly plummeted. The lady didn't pull any punches.

Justin kissed the top of Charly's head. "I know how much you want to get back out on your own. I thought you'd be happy that I found Marshall. He's the best there is."

"Yes, Daddy."

"Let me help you, Charly. Please take what I'm offering."

"I will, Daddy. Thank you."

Justin's smile was a mixture of weariness and relief. Marshall could understand the weariness. But if Justin felt relieved that Marshall would be spending time with his daughter, he was a fool.

CHAPTER THREE

"IT LIVES," BEAU TEASED when Charly entered the kitchen Monday morning.

Ignoring her brother, she grabbed the last coffee mug and stumbled toward the coffeemaker. "Shouldn't you be at work or somewhere?"

"I'm waiting for Dad."

It was only after Charly had downed a long swallow of rich black coffee that she turned toward the crowded table. All of her sisters were at the house this morning. All of them perfectly coiffed and bright-eyed.

"Good morning," Shelby said.

Charly grumbled a response and shoved some stray hair off her forehead.

"Being blown up didn't improve your personality," Beau observed as he hoisted himself onto the countertop. "I see baby sister still doesn't do mornings."

"Leave her alone, Beau," Shelby warned.

"Yeah," Charly said, topping off her coffee. "Leave me alone."

Beau tousled her hair as she moved past him. "How's the shoulder?"

"Fine," Charly lied, and gave Beau's arm a squeeze.

"You don't look fine," Marie said.

Charly took the seat across from Marie and next to

Jax. Ignoring the platter of eggs, she reached for a doughnut covered with chocolate icing and colorful sprinkles. "I'm a little sore," she admitted. "What's up?"

Shelby frowned. "Why do you think something is up?"

"There'd better be something up. Why else would you all be here? I'd hate to think you had Odelle wake me for no reason."

"It's almost nine," Marie pointed out. "You're getting lazy, little sister."

Charly sighed. "It isn't as if I have anything pressing to do."

"This little meeting was my idea," Shelby said.

"This better be good," Charly warned her.

Shelby opened her briefcase and retrieved a file folder. "I've been doing some investigating."

"On the shooting?" Charly asked hopefully. "Have you heard something about Frank's killer?"

Shelby reached out and closed her hand over Charly's. "Sorry. This has to do with the Camille Gravier murder."

Shelby handed each of them a copy of a newspaper article. As Charly began to read, she recognized the story. It was the sensationalized piece Gator Guzman had written just before Nikki's trial. The slimy reporter had done his best to draw parallels between the murder of Steven Boudreaux and that of Camille Gravier years earlier. Members of the Delacroix family had been involved in both cases.

"So?" Charly queried when she met Shelby's expectant eyes.

Her sister looked exasperated as she scanned the dining area. Apparently she'd been hoping for a more enthusiastic response from her siblings. "Don't you find this story a little disturbing?" she asked.

"I thought it was pretty tabloid at the time," Charly responded. "It probably sold a lot of papers." She watched her sister's lips purse in obvious frustration. "You aren't insinuating that you believe Grandfather had anything to do with that Camille woman's death, are you?"

Shelby gazed down at the polished wood floor. "No."

"Then I do hope you have a better reason for gathering us together than to rehash this stupid article written about a murder that took place in 1938. No one believed Gator's claims. He probably made most of this stuff up, anyway."

"I agree," Beau and Jax said in unison.

"We don't *know* that," Shelby insisted. "A lot of what Gator said was true."

"Right," Charly scoffed. "Gator's journalistic integrity is above reproach. Camille and Steven both died at the same spot on Moon Lake. I'm sure he'll be under consideration for a Pulitzer for such fine investigative reporting."

Shelby shook her head dejectedly at her sister's sarcasm. "Our great-grandfather Hamilton had some reservations during the trial. And I have some additional concerns."

"Reservations?" Marie asked.

Charly rose, refilled her coffee cup and returned to the table. "You *should* be concerned, Shelby. You're screwing up your relationship with Travis by spending so much time on this." That statement earned her a warning glare from her sisters, but Charly was undeterred.

A flash of pain flickered in Shelby's soft gray eyes. "This has nothing to do with my relationship with Travis."

"Yeah, right," Charly said. "It is his great-aunt's murder you're snooping into. I hope this isn't the reason you haven't got enough time to go to Texas with him."

Shelby ignored Charly's remark. "I've seen Hamilton's notes on the trial and something isn't right."

"Like what?" Marie asked.

"The judge, for starters."

"Alvarez?" Beau looked puzzled. "He and Hamilton were great friends."

Shelby nodded. "That friendship was strained by the trial. Hamilton made critical notes in the margins about Alvarez's rulings."

"He lost the case," Charly reminded her sister. "I'm sure he wasn't thrilled with the judge at the time."

"I think there was more to it than that," Shelby insisted. "One note mentions that Judge Alvarez would barely speak to Hamilton outside of court."

"They aren't supposed to talk outside the courtroom," Charly offered. "Ex parte communications are forbidden."

"Only about the case," Shelby said with more force than Charly thought necessary. "They were lifelong friends. Judge Alvarez was really cold to Hamilton during the trial."

Beau shrugged while Marie leaned back and took deep, relaxing breaths. Jax was silently attentive. Charly was just feeling confused. "So what if the judge was chilly? Maybe he was just keeping his distance because he knew Hamilton had a lot on his plate. After all, two of his children—Grandfather and Aunt Mary—were witnesses at the trial."

"Speaking of which," Shelby went on, "I also found a note saying Hamilton was 'getting Mary situated.' Does that mean anything to you?"

Charly sighed. "It means you've seen one too many Oliver Stone movies. Maybe he was getting Aunt Mary a comfortable seat in the courtroom. Maybe he was planning a party. Jeez, Shelby, I think you're spending too many nights alone when you could be in Texas with Travis."

"I must admit, Shelby," Marie said, "I don't see where you're going with this, either."

"Look," Shelby snapped. "I came here because I felt there was something weird about this whole case and I had hoped you guys would offer some constructive comments." She grabbed her briefcase and began tossing the copies of the article inside. "Apparently I was wrong to think any of you would be interested. Our family history doesn't seem to matter to you."

"Shelby?" Charly pleaded as her sister rose. "I'm sorry. Please don't get all bent out of shape."

Jax, Marie and Beau echoed the sentiment. Reluctantly, Shelby waited by the door, her features guarded. "I'm going to have to see Grandfather."

"About what?" Charly asked. "I don't think he'll be in any great hurry to read Gator's article again. He wasn't exactly thrilled when Gator printed that stuff about him dating Camille."

Marie agreed. "He did seem hurt. It's probably understandable if he was fond of the woman. I can't imagine being a witness to the murder of someone I knew. Especially not at twenty."

"I need to know why Hamilton lost the case."

"Because Rafe Perdido was guilty?" Beau suggested.

"Maybe," Shelby answered. "I'd like to know why Camille ended up dead in Moon Lake."

Charly shrugged. "It doesn't matter now. The poor woman is long gone."

"It matters," Shelby insisted.

"Why?" Jax asked.

"Because Camille was pregnant when she was killed."

Charly and her siblings exchanged hushed words of surprise. "How do you know that?"

"Travis told me."

Charly's mind was racing even before she dared to ask the question. "You don't think she and Grandfather were...lovers, do you?"

"I didn't say that," Shelby answered quickly. "But I hope now you all understand that there may be more going on here than we realized at first. I sure wasn't looking for any of this when Toni gave me these files to return to Grandfather's office. I suppose if I hadn't read them and just slipped them into Delacroix and Associates archives, I wouldn't feel so compelled to unearth old history. But the fact is that I did read Hamilton's personal notes on the case—the only murder case he ever lost, remember—and there are just too many things that don't make sense.''

Charly shook her head. "I don't see it," she stated emphatically. "If I'm understanding your innuendo, you're suggesting that our grandfather murdered Camille and then our great-grandfather Hamilton somehow allowed Rafe Perdido to be convicted for the crime. No way, Shelby.''

"I didn't say that," Shelby insisted, knowing that it was probably the truth. "I'm just saying that there are too many inconsistencies and half-truths.''

Charly leaned back, mulling over all that Shelby had said. "Maybe Grandfather was involved.''

"Charly!" her siblings railed.

"Hear me out," she countered. "Gator's article said that Rafe knew Camille and that Granddad was dating her. Maybe Rafe was jealous and killed Camille because she dumped him. It makes sense. Camille was drowned, which is definitely a crime-of-passion killing. Maybe he found out she was pregnant, they fought, and he killed her.

"However," Charly went on, "if you're asking me, I can't believe Grandfather was a randy stud." She shivered. "I don't even want to think about him doing...*it*. Ever.''

"Well, I'd like to know the truth," Shelby said.

Charly felt a sudden surge of empathy for her sister. Lord knew, she would give anything to find out what had happened the night Frank was killed. "What can we do to help?''

Shelby seemed to relax. "I'm not sure yet, but I would appreciate it if all of you kept quiet about what

I've just told you. Especially don't say anything to Aunt Mary."

"You got it," Charly agreed. "If you need any leg-work done, give me a call."

"I will," Shelby said. "Now I've got to slip back into lawyer mode and get to the office before Grandfather wonders where I am."

Jax and her twin, Beau, headed off to the stables and Marie rose, too.

"I've got to get back to the store," she announced. "Lucas said to call him if you have any problems with your shoulder, Charly. I made you a massage oil for the pain."

"Thanks," Charly said, and watched her siblings file out of the house.

It was times like this that made her long for the peace and quiet of her apartment in Slidell. She loved her family, but she missed her privacy dearly. With her finger, she scraped a huge blob of frosting off another doughnut and popped it into her mouth.

"Are you really going to eat that?" Avery asked, suddenly appearing in the doorway.

She met his intense gaze. "Excuse me?"

"Empty calories," he explained. "If you expect your body to heal properly, you have to give it the right fuel."

He looked fit and healthy in running shorts and a T-shirt that left very little of his impressive body to her imagination. "This *is* the right fuel. I can't start the day without the appropriate infusion of caffeine and chocolate."

He gave her the same look a parent might offer a

wayward child. "I see I have my work cut out for me with you."

"You can quit anytime," she suggested sweetly.

He moved past her to the refrigerator as if he'd been in residence forever. Charly knew she shouldn't stare, but she couldn't help it. It should be illegal for a man to look that good so early in the morning. His legs were muscular and tanned. Running shorts hugged his tapered hips, and just a hint of his flat stomach was revealed when he sauntered back to the table.

Charly told herself that the sudden rush in her system was because of the chocolate. "*What* is that?"

Avery began slicing a banana into a bowl filled with rubbery white cubes. "Tofu. Want some?"

"I don't eat anything that looks like a science project."

He smiled. "It's soybean curd—just loaded with protein."

"I think I'll stick with hamburgers, thanks."

He tilted his head to one side. "Your father didn't tell me I'd also have to educate you on proper nutrition."

"Don't bother," Charly said. "I stopped believing in the nutrition fairy when I discovered Twinkies."

"Twinkies?"

She sighed. "Food of the gods. They're a whole lot more appetizing than that stuff."

Avery sprinkled what looked like birdseed into the bowl. Charly went to refill her coffee cup.

"Have you ever heard of moderation?" he asked.

"I'm a cop," she answered. "I'm supposed to drink coffee by the gallon and eat doughnuts nonstop."

"Not every cop has a garbage disposal for a stomach."

"This one does," she informed him. "I don't like to eat anything I haven't unwrapped."

His laughter brought a smile to her lips. The man was truly charming and—consequently—extremely dangerous. Charly reminded herself that she wasn't in the same league.

"What was the private meeting all about?"

"How did you know we had a private meeting?"

His broad shoulders lifted in a slight shrug. "Odelle warned me to wait until I heard the others leave."

Charly smiled. "Did she wake you up, too?"

"Who?"

"Odelle."

"I've been up for hours. I've already set up the weights in the old tack room and I've mapped out a trail for our run."

"Our run?"

He flashed that killer grin. "We'll build up your cardiovascular endurance to get the most out of your workouts."

Charly groaned. "I hate to run and I've never been real hot on lifting weights."

"You sure are full of complaints, darlin'."

"I'm a lot nicer after noon," she grumbled, heading for the door. "Ask anyone."

"Where are you going?"

Charly didn't turn around. "Back to bed."

"No, you're not. Get changed and we'll meet out front in ten minutes."

"We can meet out front in two hours," she informed him tersely. "I was up until three."

"Couldn't sleep?"

It's not that I can't. I'm afraid to go to sleep. "I got caught up in an old movie."

"Which one?"

Charly turned to face him. "*Princess O'Rourke*. I'm sure you've never—"

"Olivia de Havilland, 1943?"

"You've seen it?" She was truly shocked.

Avery laced his fingers and placed them behind his head, his biceps flexing with the action. Charly reminded herself that men like Marshall Avery weren't interested in women like her. *Then why do I keep getting the feeling that he's flirting with me?*

"I happen to like old movies," he explained.

"Really?"

"Yes. Does that surprise you?"

Charly shrugged. "Maybe. You strike me as the mindless-action-flick type."

"Ouch," he teased, placing one hand over his heart. "A mortal wound to the ego."

Charly smiled. "Something tells me your ego will survive. I'll see you after a while."

"Ten minutes, or I'm coming up to get you."

"Forget it, Avery. I need some sleep."

"Regular exercise promotes peaceful sleep."

"You sound like a bad fortune cookie. Later!"

"EITHER YOU PUT IT ON, or you don't run."

Charly glared up at him. "You aren't a very likable guy, Avery."

"Neither are you," he answered smoothly.

Charly bristled, then grabbed the sling from his hand. Slipping one of the straps over her head, she gingerly cradled her arm in the cotton pouch.

"Turn around."

Jump. Sit. Speak. She silently fumed.

She felt his knuckles brush her back and she knew without question that she would burn in hell for her thoughts.

"Be still," he grumbled.

"Easy for you to say," Charly whispered.

"It wouldn't be this hot if you'd listened to me and we'd gotten out here earlier," he said, adjusting the sling. "We'll probably dehydrate and get sunstroke in the first quarter-mile."

"I'm all for bagging this," she offered. "Jogging was your idea. I never walk when I can drive."

Avery gave her a stern look, but his eyes flashed with amusement. "Let's warm up."

"Let's," she agreed without enthusiasm.

She followed him to one of the huge white columns that dominated the front porch.

Avery brushed his fingers over the scarred wood. "Was this you?" he asked.

Charly grinned devilishly. "I was eight years old when I carved my initials there with a steak knife. My mother sent me to my room until I was thirty."

"Let's start with some stretching," Avery suggested as he sat on the ground and extended one leg forward. Charly followed his lead, mimicking his actions even though her out-of-condition body gave loud and instantaneous protest. "How long were you actually punished?"

"Two days."

"That explains a lot."

"What is that supposed to mean?"

"Flex your toes as you lean forward. Don't bounce. Keep the motion smooth." He switched positions to stretch his other leg. "I get the feeling that you lack proper discipline."

Charly scoffed. "My parents didn't believe in spanking."

"What's it like to come from such a big family?"

"Loud," she answered, reaching for the hand he held out to her. The simple act of touching her hand was perfectly innocent. So why did she feel so guilty? Why was she noticing things like the line of dark hair that disappeared into the waistband of his shorts? Why did the strength of his touch cause a burning in the pit of her stomach?

"Why loud?"

"There were so many of us, and we Delacroix are born with strong opinions."

"Ready?"

"I'd really rather not," Charly breathed.

"I'm sure," he said, motioning for her to lead the way.

They hadn't even made it to the end of the drive and already Charly was bathed in perspiration. The early afternoon sun was little more than a faint yellowish light, masked by the thick gray haze of humidity.

"I thought swimming was good exercise," she suggested, battling to keep pace with his long, easy strides.

"It is. We can add swimming to our regimen."

"Instead of adding, why don't we replace running with swimming."

"Stop being such a baby," he chided.

"I'm not a baby. I just think running is a stupid form of activity. Especially when it has to be near ninety degrees out here."

"I warned you that running in the morning would be easier. You went back to bed."

"I'm recovering from being shot," Charly snapped. "You make it sound like I was lying in bed munching on peeled grapes."

"How did it happen?"

Charly turned her head to look at his profile. She was again taken by his earthy good looks. The man didn't seem to be struggling in the least. Each movement was like a celebration of motion.

"I was shot on duty."

"Tough break," he said.

"It was for my partner. He died."

"Have they caught the shooter?"

A little prick of warning went off in her brain. "Shooter? Did you pick up the lingo from cop shows?"

He veered off onto the path that led to the lake. "Lucas said your shoulder was just bruised in the explosion at the wedding. It shouldn't slow down our training routine. You'll be back on track in no time."

Interesting change of subject, Charly thought. "I have to be better than back on track. I have to be perfect."

"Why is that?"

"Because Chief Harrington is in no hurry to have me back. The chief and almost all of the officers in the Slidell PD think I'm responsible for Frank's death."

"Why?"

"Because it's true."

CHAPTER FOUR

"WHAT IS THAT SUPPOSED to mean?"

Charly slowed her pace. "Nothing."

He slowed, as well. "Doesn't sound like nothing."

"Skip it, Avery. You ask a lot of questions. Are you writing a book?"

He smiled. "If you kiss me, we can call it a love story."

The image of being kissed by Avery was almost enough to cause her to stumble on the uneven pathway. "Don't do that."

"Do what?"

"Flirt with me."

"Why not?"

Charly slowed to a stop, then bent forward, her breath coming in a series of labored gasps. "I'm dying here, Avery. There has to be a better way to go about this."

"We can turn back now," he said. "But just this once. You'll never be super cop if you peter out after only two miles."

Charly willed herself a second wind. "I'm a patrol officer. I patrol in a car, not on foot. I hate to run."

"You complain a lot."

"So you said." The sun's rays felt like a torch between her shoulder blades. "And I've said on more than one occasion that you were welcome to quit."

"I've never quit before, darlin'."

"I guess not," she said. "You picked a pretty cushy profession."

"Cushy?"

"I hate to think what my father is paying you. It's probably more than I make in a year, if your watch and running shoes are any indication. Not to mention great perks like moving into our house with free room and board. Seems pretty cushy to me."

"You forgot something."

Charly lifted her eyes to meet his. "What?"

"A great view."

"Bayou Beltane is a beautiful place to live."

"I wasn't talking about the landscape."

Charly blushed furiously and averted her gaze. "Please stop that."

He laughed. "I can't help it. You make it too easy."

Charly was about to respond when an approaching police car caught her attention. The car slowed to a stop as the driver pulled up next to them.

"Hey, Charly."

"Hey, Digger," she greeted. Digger's smile was punctuated by boyish dimples in the baby fat that had never left him. "What are you doing all the way out here?"

"Came to see how you were," he said, mopping his brow on the sleeve of his uniform. "The trouble at the wedding is all anyone's talking about. Incidentally, that woman from the catering service is out of the woods. Who's your friend?"

"Digger DuMonde, this is Marshall Avery. Do me a favor and arrest him for battery."

"Say what?" Digger asked, scratching his head. "This boy bothering you?"

Charly looked from the pudgy officer to Avery. Somehow the word *boy* didn't fit. "I was joking, Digger. Avery is my personal trainer."

Digger smiled. "You mean like them TV stars got?"

"I was thinking more along the lines of marine boot camp."

"A healthy body is important," Avery said, offering his hand. "Nice to meet you, Digger. Just ignore her, she's a complainer."

Digger sucked in his gut and puffed out his chest as the two men shook hands. "My pleasure, Mr. Avery. So, little Charly is giving you sass?"

Avery sighed. "She is that. Contrary little thing."

"The next person who uses 'little' in a sentence will be picking his teeth off the ground."

Digger chuckled. "Sorry. Pay attention, son. She may look small but I've seen her hold her own in a fight."

"Fight?" Avery repeated, one dark brow arching.

The amusement tugging the corners of his mouth made her long to sucker punch him. "I always liked to think of it as attitude adjustment," Charly informed him.

"The last guy she…adjusted…needed five stitches."

Avery gaped at Charly, then turned back to Digger. "You're exaggerating, right?"

"Okay, so maybe it was only four."

"The guy was being less than a gentleman to his date, so I intervened."

"He must not have been much of a man if you subdued him," Avery said.

"He was a big one," Digger insisted. "Two, two fifty, wouldn't you say, Charly?"

"I didn't think about his weight at the time," Charly said, deciding it was time to change the subject. "How are things down at the station?"

Digger shrugged. "I miss you."

"You're the only one."

Digger placed his hat back on his head. "It will settle down soon, Charly. Once you get back and show them guys what you can do, everything else will work out."

"I hope so, Digger, and thanks. I'd give you a kiss but I don't think you want me near you right now."

"I gotta run, anyhow," he said. "Shift starts in an hour. Take care, and I'm glad you're okay. I was real worried when I heard you'd taken another hit to that shoulder."

"It isn't as bad as it looks," she said, running her fingers over her arm. "The sling was his idea. So was running around in the heat of the day."

Digger laughed. "I sure as hell didn't think it was yours. Take care now, hear?"

"You, too."

With a wave, Digger backed in between two pine trees, then turned out onto the road. His tires spewed out dust as he headed toward the road to Slidell.

"I never would have pegged you as a brawler."

"Leave it alone," Charly warned. "And don't you

dare repeat that story in front of Daddy. No charges were laid, but Daddy was *not* pleased when he found out about it.''

"Rest time is over, pick up the pace."

"Goody," she muttered as she forced herself into a slow jog. "I'm going to soak the rest of the day."

"Not hardly," he said. "We have weights and strengthening work still ahead of us."

"C'mon, Avery! Aren't you supposed to build up to these things? Why don't you take the rest of the day and haunt some of your other clients?"

"I don't have any other clients. I'm all yours."

"WHAT IS THAT?"

Charly twirled and looked at him with wide, surprised eyes. After chewing and swallowing, she quickly put one hand behind her back. "What?"

He took two steps toward her, not stopping until they were toe-to-toe. His intention had been to intimidate. But like many grand intentions, it fell by the wayside as soon as he caught the floral fragrance of her still-damp hair.

"This," he said in a soft voice as he reached out and pressed his thumb to the corner of her slightly parted lips. Her skin was soft, and her little puffs of breath were warm and welcome. His body reacted fiercely and instantly. Touching Charly Delacroix was like touching some sort of exotic goddess. She was such a contradiction that his interest was well past piqued.

Marshall took his time wiping the smear from her lips. Slowly and deliberately, he kept his gaze fixed on hers while his thumb molded her pliant flesh. Her eyes changed as he drew out the touch. Watching them intensify was like watching a violent summer squall approach. By the time he finally pulled away, his breathing was uneven. But so was hers.

"This," he repeated, showing her the smudge of chocolate.

"Oh, that," she hedged. "You said I should eat five small meals a day."

"I don't recall telling you that chocolate cake constituted a meal."

"Then you've probably never had a Ring-Ding. They're very filling."

She skittered over to the table, and he found himself amused and intrigued when he noticed the slight tremor in her hand. She headed toward the stairs. "I'd better change if we're going to do the weights."

Marshall allowed his eyes to roam over her small body. Faded cutoffs hugged her firm derriere and revealed almost all of her shapely legs. In spite of her avowed aversion to exercise, she was in terrific condition. Maybe too terrific.

"Care to explain this little scene?"

Marshall turned toward the voice and found Beau framed in the kitchen doorway, his arms crossed in front of his chest. Even in an expensive suit, the man looked ready and willing to do battle.

"I was only looking," Marshall said, and he raised his hands, palms out.

Beau's dark head fell to one side, and his gray eyes narrowed menacingly. "Charly is off-limits."

Marshall nodded. "I agree."

Beau stared for a few more seconds before offering a barely perceptible nod of his head. "Step out of line and I'll hurt you."

"Why don't we let Charly decide if I cross the line?"

Beau was on him in a flash. Marshall expelled a breath as he was pushed against the wall. He knew full well that it wouldn't take much to send Beau sailing across the room. But he also knew that he wouldn't be in his present predicament if he hadn't baited the man. Hell, he wasn't even sure what had made him do it.

"Jeez, Beau! What are you doing?" Charly yelled as she raced back into the kitchen and wriggled between them. "Back off!"

Somewhat grudgingly, Beau released Marshall. "You're fired."

Marshall smiled slowly. "I don't think so. Justin hired me. I'll have to hear it from him."

"Will one of you two barbarians please tell me what this is all about?" Charly said.

Beau straightened his jacket. "Your personal trainer is putting a little too much emphasis on the personal. He was ogling you as if—"

"So what?" Charly shook her head. "For heaven's sake, Beau. He was looking at my legs. Do you think no man has ever looked at me before?"

Marshall was surprised by her frankness.

"Not in front of me, they haven't," Beau shot back. "And this guy happens to be sleeping in the room next to you!"

"Well," Charly began, moving right up against

Beau, "save your big brother act for when he's sleeping *in* my room."

Beau turned red with rage. "Don't even think about it," he warned Marshall.

"Go to work, Beau. I can handle Avery."

Don't be so sure, Marshall thought. For some reason it rankled to know that Charly could dismiss him so casually. It was like a gauntlet tossed at his feet. He was still trying to decide if he should pick it up when the telephone rang.

Charly picked up the receiver. "Hello?"

He watched her face as she listened. He saw shock, annoyance and just a little bit of fear.

"I'll be right there."

"Something wrong?"

Charly was still holding the receiver when she looked up at him. Blinking once, then twice, she said, "Someone broke into my apartment."

"Why would anyone do that?" Beau asked. "That place is a hovel."

"I've got to go over there," Charly said, ignoring her brother's remark.

"No, you don't," Beau argued. "I've got a meeting in a little while. I'll take you over there when I get back from New Orleans."

"I'm going now."

"I'll ride with her," Marshall suggested.

Grudgingly, Beau nodded. "Call me and let me know how bad it is."

He had to yell the final few words because Charly had dashed out of the kitchen in search of her keys.

Beau eyed him warily. "Remember what I said," he warned before leaving.

"Forget what he said." Charly's voice arrived a split second before she burst into the room. "If you're coming, let's go."

Marshall followed her from the house. "Hey!" he called as she opened the door to the red convertible. "You're upset and racing around in a dozen directions. I'd feel better if you let me drive."

She tossed him the keys and slid across the driver's seat. "Hurry up."

Marshall got in, moved the seat back and started the engine. In no time, he had the little sports car speeding toward Slidell.

"I'm sorry about Beau," she said.

Marshall shrugged. "No harm done."

"He can't help it if he's a jerk. He was born that way."

"He wasn't being a jerk. He was only trying to look out for his baby sister. That's why I didn't kick his butt."

Charly laughed. "You'd better be careful. Beau is in really great shape. I don't think he's ever lost a fight."

"Does he fight often?"

"Not anymore. But he was a real hellion when he was younger."

"I hear some hero worship in there."

He glanced over and saw her faint blush. "Don't say anything to Beau. He already has a huge ego."

"Really?"

"Sure. Beau is quite...popular in these parts." She

shifted and tucked one tanned leg beneath her. "He admits that he *loves* women."

"Nice sentiment."

"Except that with my brother it isn't a sentiment, it's a way of life. You see, Beau loves all women, and he feels it's his duty to tell each one personally."

Marshall laughed. "I get the picture. So, how did you know I was looking at your legs?"

She shrugged and fixed her eyes on the road ahead of them. "It was a guess. But I know Beau blew everything out of proportion and I'm sorry for that."

"Come again?"

"You're a hopeless flirt, Avery, but we both know men like you aren't interested in women like me."

He checked his grin. "We're not?"

"Men who look like you are only interested in women like my friend Jada."

"Was there a compliment buried in there somewhere?"

"Just an observation. I'm sure you know you're gorgeous. You don't need to hear it from me."

But I'd like to. "That whoosh of air you just heard was my ego deflating."

Her laughter was soft and incredibly sexy. That, coupled with the feline way she rubbed against her seat, had his mind wandering to places he knew it shouldn't go. Not if he was going to carry off his charade.

"Is that why you hang out with Jada?"

"Jada is my friend."

"I'm sure she is," he responded quickly. "But I think you use Jada like a shield. The same way you've trained your brother. Between the two of them, I'll bet a man never gets within ten feet of you."

"Don't be silly," Charly protested. "I may not have the allure of Jada or my sisters, but I'm not exactly a double-bagger, either."

"You're definitely not that," he agreed smoothly. "And you're wrong about your allure, Charly."

"You just crossed that fine line between flirting and lying, Avery. Take the next exit."

Marshall didn't press her. The knowledge that she really believed she wasn't a smart, witty, beautiful woman stunned him.

He continued to follow her directions until they came upon four marked police units parked at odd angles in front of an old converted home.

Charly bounded from the car the instant it stopped. He followed on her heels, weaving in and out of the small crowd, then beneath the yellow crime scene tape.

"Well, well, Delacroix," a burly officer posted at the door said as he moved his hulking frame to block their path. "With you in the area, do I call in tactical alert for snipers?"

"Go to hell, Johnson," Charly said, and turned sideways to pass by him.

"Can't let you in, Delacroix. Law enforcement personnel only, and we both know you don't have what that takes. Frank died learning that lesson."

Marshall stepped forward and grabbed the man in his most vulnerable spot. "Apologize or I'll squeeze hard enough to make you sing soprano."

"Delacroix?"

"Out here, Chief!" Charly called.

A lanky man wearing a crisp white uniform shirt and the air of authority stepped forward. His badge read Harrington, Chief. "What the hell is going on here?"

Marshall glanced at the newcomer. "I was just giving Officer Johnson some singing lessons."

Chief Harrington's brow furrowed. "Come on inside," he said to Charly. "We'll need a list of what's missing."

Marshall released the officer and followed Charly into the building. He heard her give a little cry, and he understood why as soon as he took a look at her first-floor apartment, or what was left of it.

Officers were crawling all over the place, looking like ants in their black uniforms. Conversation in the living room stopped the instant Charly's arrival was noted. It soon became obvious to Marshall that every member of the department, except for the chief, harbored real hostility toward the woman. Feeling uncharacteristically protective, he draped his arm around her shoulder and steered her through the chaos that had once been her home.

There wasn't a drawer or cabinet that hadn't been emptied. The sofa was toppled and the cushions slit. Everything seemed to be bathed in a fine coating of downy feathers.

"This isn't your typical B and E," he said against her ear.

Charly seemed numb as she stepped over videotapes, papers and pieces of splintered wood. Marshall's hand was still on her shoulder as they entered the hallway.

"Ever guess that Delacroix was hiding all this sexy

stuff under her uniform? Hell, I might just have to give it to her the next time I see her."

Marshall felt a blinding rage as he entered the bedroom and found the source of the rude comment. A young cop with a bulk of steroid-enhanced muscles was sitting on the edge of the upturned mattress, a pair of black lace panties dangling from his fingertips.

"Glad you like them, Bill," Charly said. "Keep them if you want. I've heard you're into that sort of thing."

Bill tossed the panties down as if they had suddenly caught fire. "Watch your mouth, Delacroix."

"Good advice," Marshall said, stepping forward. "If you're finished groping her lingerie, take a hike."

"Listen, boy," Bill warned. "You—"

"Bill! Gary!" the chief called. "Let's go."

Bill walked toward the doorway, where the chief now stood. He paused only long enough to say, "We aren't finished here, boy."

"Anytime," Marshall promised.

"Look at this," Charly wailed. "Some of my clothes have been cut."

"The lab boys will need those," Chief Harrington said. "For now, just make a list of what you know is missing. I'll leave Johnson by the front door."

"This isn't a simple robbery," Charly said. "Whoever did this was majorly pissed at me."

"Any ideas?" Harrington asked.

Charly looked from the chief to Marshall, then back to the chief. "I haven't spent a night here in months. You know I've been staying at Riverwood since my...accident."

Harrington scratched the front of his bald spot. "Have you had any trouble lately?"

"Other than the bomb that blew up at Joanna's wedding?" Charly returned smartly.

Harrington looked properly chastised. "The FBI thinks that incident was the work of some fringe group trying to make a statement since your father is a federal judge and your great-uncle is a state senator. I'll give them a heads-up on this, though, just in case there's some sort of connection."

"Thanks."

"Anything else?" Harrington prompted. "Have a tiff with a boyfriend? Anything?"

"Nothing," Charly said, though she no longer maintained eye contact. "I can't believe I even know anyone who would do something like this."

Marshall left Charly alone under the pretense of giving her some privacy. Back in the living room, he began sifting through the debris. The only thing that was even moderately interesting was a magazine opened to a quiz on how to enjoy sex with your ideal man. He smiled. Charly's score indicated that she should consider becoming a nun.

He tossed the magazine aside and went to the apartment door. No scratches in the paint or around the lock. He checked the windows and found nothing there.

"I think I should just get a can of gasoline and torch the place," Charly said when she emerged from the bedroom. "I don't know what's worse, *thinking* about a total stranger being in here or *knowing* that Bill was."

"He seemed like a nice fellow," Marshall observed dryly. "After meeting a few of your fellow officers, I must say I fail to understand why you want to go back to work with them.''

"Because it's what I worked hard for. Ever since I left Tulane, all I ever wanted was to be a cop.''

"Sorry you made that decision?''

"Nope,'' she answered without hesitation. Charly plucked some videotapes off the floor. "I would have made a lousy lawyer.''

"You were pre-law?''

"Second-year law,'' she corrected.

Marshall studied her profile. "You bailed out a year shy of your law degree?''

She cocked her head and gave him an icy glare. "I have enough people giving me grief about my vocational choice that I'll thank you to keep your opinion to yourself.''

"Just a question,'' Marshall said. "Sorry.''

Charly let out an audible breath, and tucked the videos under her arm. "I can't find a single thing missing.''

"No money or jewelry?''

"I don't have either,'' she answered.

He gave her a playful wink. "Then someone went to an awful lot of trouble for nothing.''

"Let's go,'' she said.

Marshall saw the flicker of pain in her eyes before she snapped a mask of nonchalance into place. He wasn't sure if the brave front was for his benefit or for the officers still lingering in the parking lot.

He noted that none of Slidell's finest bothered to say goodbye. They stared at Charly as if she were a pariah. She didn't let on that it bothered her. But it sure as hell bothered him. He hadn't known her very long, but he knew without question that Charly Delacroix would never stand by and do nothing while another officer was gunned down. Never.

"Home?" he asked, once they were in the car and he inserted the key into the ignition.

Charly didn't open her eyes. She sat against the seat, clutching the videos to her chest, and muttered, "Sure."

Marshall backtracked to the highway, replaying the scene in his mind. Whoever had broken into her place must have had a key or else were professionals.

"What kind of things did you work on before you were shot?"

"What?"

"I was just wondering what kind of cases you handled before you were shot."

Charly shrugged. "I wasn't on the force long enough to get a case. Unless you count Ray Don driving drunk."

"But your friend—Digger—he said you broke up a fight?"

"That was back when I was in the academy. I worked for the New Orleans PD as a computer analyst then."

"Did you ever come across anything that might have made you an enemy?"

Charly was quiet for a minute, then she said, "Rico Tesconti."

"Rico Tesconti of the Garibaldi crime family?" he asked.

"The one and only. How come you know who Tesconti is?"

He glanced at her and winked. "I might be a lowly personal trainer, but I read the papers and watch TV."

"Sorry," she mumbled. "I helped the task force with a computer program that tracked Tesconti's financial records. He beat the indictment, though. So I can't believe he'd waste his time with me. The man is virtually untouchable even though he has a hand in every illegal enterprise in New Orleans."

"What about when you were on duty in Slidell?"

"Frank and I did five traffic stops. We answered a call at Swampy's the night before the shooting."

"The same place where you were shot?"

"Yes."

"What happened?"

"Frank went inside first. He told me to stay by the door while he looked for a guy who was supposed to be there."

"Who was this guy?"

Charly jabbed her fingers against her temples. "O'Bannon...O'Grady. I'm not sure, but he wasn't there."

"You're positive?"

Charly laughed. "Since Frank and I were the only ones in the place who spoke English, I'm basically certain that there wasn't a redheaded, green-eyed Irish national in the bar."

"What kind of place is Swampy's?"

"A hole in the wall that caters to migrant workers." At his blank look, she continued, "For ones who come to Louisiana and the rest of the South when the crops come in. Of course, if you were really from the South, you'd have known that. Where are you from, Avery?"

"Here and there."

"Nice try," she breathed. "Either tell me or I'll have to resort to sneaking your fingerprints and running a complete background check on you."

"You won't find anything," he said. That much was true.

"C'mon, Avery. You—"

The shrill chirp of her car phone sounded and Charly's knuckles brushed against him as she reached to put the call on speaker, knowing full well it had to be her brother.

"Hi, Beau," she said before the caller could speak. "I know it's you. Sorry I forgot to call you. My stuff is pretty much trashed, right down to the furniture. Don't tell Daddy, okay?" She waited a moment but there was no reply. "Beau? Are you there? What's wrong?"

"The time is right, Charly."

"Who is this?" she demanded. "What are you talking about?"

"The time is right for you to die."

CHAPTER FIVE

"HOW LONG?" MARSHALL demanded once he had pulled the car onto the shoulder of the highway, heedless of the incensed drivers honking at them.

Charly actually trembled at the barely contained fury in his voice. "I've been getting the calls since I came out of a coma and they moved me to a private room. It's nothing."

"That didn't sound like nothing to me," he shouted, his fingers biting into the flesh of her upper arms. "Why in hell didn't you tell Harrington about these calls?"

"Because," she began, shrugging out of his grasp, "I'm sure that is exactly what they want me to do."

"Who is they?"

"One of my fellow officers. I'm sure they think that they can scare me off."

Marshall angrily swept his hair back off his forehead, then dropped his hands to the steering wheel. "A bomb is planted in your car, your apartment is trashed, and you don't think there's a connection?"

"Of course there's a connection," Charly told him. "I mean, I think the same person who made the calls trashed my place. I doubt he planted the bomb, though."

"Why?"

"Because they're cops, Avery. They want to scare me, not kill me. I'm the only woman on the force, and they blame me for Frank's death."

"Your caller didn't sound like he was too interested in affirmative action. You've got to go to the cops."

"Back off, Avery," she warned. "Every prominent socialite and politician for two hundred miles around was at Joanna and Logan's wedding. I'm sure the FBI knows what it's doing, and they think it was just some crackpot extremist making a statement."

"Extremists don't explode bombs and keep mum. If it was some radical group, they would have called every newspaper and television station to take credit."

Quietly, she searched his face, noting the concern and determination in the set of his jaw. "Who *are* you?"

There was just a brief flicker of something in his eyes before he flashed a bone-melting smile. "I'm your trainer."

"Don't treat me like a fool, Avery. You appear out of nowhere and all these weird things start happening to me. I'm not pointing the finger at you, I just want to know what your game really is. And don't try to tell me you're nothing but a jock with a passion for current events and police shows."

"You want to know what my passions are?" he murmured as he leaned across the console. His eyes were riveted to her mouth.

Charly suddenly found it difficult to breathe. The heat she was feeling had absolutely nothing to do with air temperature and everything to do with him. "I can guess," she said evenly.

"Why trouble your imagination when you can have the real thing?" he suggested.

She had expected a kiss, was even braced for it. She wasn't at all prepared for the gentle nibble he gave her lower lip. Nor was she prepared for the way his eyes were locked on hers, fairly daring her to protest.

Charly never backed down from anything. Flattening her palms against his chest, she tilted her head back, forcing him to relinquish her lip. As soon as he did so, she brushed a kiss on his open mouth that was little more than a whisper. It was meant to provoke.

But it backfired. Big-time. Marshall's hands glided up along her throat until her face rested in his palms. He shifted her beneath his mouth, taking control and mastering her with a mere kiss. No, not a mere kiss—it was seduction.

He tasted hot and faintly of mint as his tongue flicked out to toy with her lip. The action was so simple yet so erotic that Charly swallowed the moan rumbling up from her stomach. How had she gotten herself into this mess in the first place?

For several torturous moments, she ignored the sensuous circles his thumbs made against her cheeks. She ignored the solid heat of his chest. Ignored the wanton invitation of his kiss.

Her lack of response worked rather well. As soon as he realized that she no longer moved beneath him, that her lips had become a tight seam, he lifted his head.

She braced herself for a barrage of insults, and heaven knew she deserved them. What was she thinking to kiss a man like Avery with such abandon and aggression? It had to be the heat.

When she finally mustered the courage to look at him, she found him wearing a huge grin. ''What's so funny?'' she snapped.

''I like the way you look when you're all rumpled and manhandled.''

Marshall reached out and in a wickedly sensual motion ran his fingertip across her lower lip, then lifted it to his own mouth for one final taste of her.

Charly sat back in the seat, trying to regain some control over her raging pulse. Playing with Avery was like playing with fire, and she knew with certainty that she would get burned. Lord, the man could turn a simple kiss into a carnal experience!

''Promise me you won't say anything to Daddy or Beau,'' she said after they had driven in silence for several miles.

''I value my life too much to risk telling your brother or your father that I kissed you.''

''Not the kiss,'' Charly said. ''I mean the calls. I left Jax's cabin because I wanted them to stop.''

''At least talk to the FBI agent investigating the bombing.''

''Promise you won't say anything?''

''What's in it for me?'' he teased.

''Promise me, Avery.''

''I have a name, you know.''

''I know. I just don't like it.''

''My parents did.''

''Fine,'' she said, feeling some of the tension begin

to ease from her gut. "Then your parents can call you by your name. I'll stick to Avery."

"You'll say it one day."

"Not on your life."

He reached over and gave her thigh a quick squeeze. "We'll see."

"I JUST WANT TO KNOW where you found him."

Justin pressed his fingertips together and regarded her from across his desk. That action was enough to remind Charly of those oft-repeated lectures from her early childhood. She was summoned to her father's office on a regular basis for her many misdemeanors—unlike her older sisters.

"Is there something about him that you don't like?"

Charly rose and paced behind the hand-stitched leather chair. "Not exactly. I just want to know more about him."

"He's a personal trainer, Charly. I contacted him on a referral."

"From whom?" she pressed.

Justin sighed. "I got the name from the wife of one of my associates. I called and he agreed to come here to work with you. Look, Charly, is there something you don't like about Marshall? Has he behaved inappropriately?"

"No, Daddy. I just want some background information."

Justin seemed to run out of patience. "Are you doubting my judgment? Don't you think I looked into this man's past before I brought him here to help you?"

"Yes, Daddy."

"I have never agreed with your decision to leave law school, but I tried to understand your motives."

"I appreciate that."

"I couldn't understand your decision to place yourself in danger as a police officer, but I have tried to be supportive."

"I know that, Daddy."

"Because I know how much it means to you to get back to work, I brought Marshall to Bayou Beltane. I did this in spite of my personal feelings and misgivings, and I am genuinely hurt that you look upon my actions with suspicion."

"I'm really thankful, Daddy. I'm sorry if I sounded ungrateful."

Justin came around and gently pulled Charly into his arms. He smelled faintly of cologne and his silk-blended shirt was soft and warm where she rested her cheek. The feel of the material and the familiar scent threw her back to her earlier childhood. Back to when she felt like the treasured child of loving parents. Before everything fell apart.

She left Justin's office a few minutes later, silently berating herself for letting her father do it to her again. He had this magical way of twisting every conversation so that she ended up apologizing. She went up to her room with the weight of their many unspoken conflicts bouncing around in her head. And her relationship with her mother was strained, as well. She still couldn't forgive Madeline for taking her away from her father ten years ago. Just as she couldn't forgive her father for so many years of nothing but cards and professionally wrapped presents with hastily scribbled notes.

Remembering those painful years made Charly reluctant to attempt sleep. It was early yet, and Avery had told her he was an old-movie buff.

"Let's test him and see," she whispered, and bypassed her own door for his.

Charly leaned her head forward so that her ear rested against the cool surface of the wood. She didn't hear any sound and wondered if he might be asleep. She also wondered if she had an ulterior motive. The fact that the mere memory of his kiss could curl her toes had nothing to do with the fact that she was standing outside his bedroom door at midnight.

Gathering her nerve, she knocked, once, then twice. She listened again, then had a thought.

Placing her hand on the knob, she was a little surprised to find the door locked. Surprised but undeterred.

Charly ran back to her room and opened her closet. She found her set of lock picks where she had left them, in her riding boots. Opening the leather case, she selected the tapered tool she knew would work on the old lock.

She dismissed the twinge of conscience that struck as she knelt in front of Avery's door. If he wouldn't tell her anything about himself, she'd just take matters into her own hands—literally.

The lock slipped in the course of seconds and Charly soundlessly entered the room. She stood perfectly still until her heart rate returned to normal and her eyes adjusted to the partial darkness.

Then she heard muffled voices.

Moving to the open window, she carefully peeked around the curtain into the trees that lined the pool area. She recognized Avery immediately. His companion was another story. She could tell it was a woman even before she watched the silhouetted figure move to give him a kiss on the cheek.

Charly backed away from the window. She had no desire to watch Avery seduce some other woman in the moonlight. She didn't even want to think about it.

But she couldn't help it. Knowing what it felt like to share a kiss with Avery was too fresh, too powerful. "He's got a girlfriend," she whispered as she went to the closet and opened the double doors. "Figures."

His clothing hung in neat order, like items placed together. Charly yanked the overhead chain to flood the small area with light. Running her hands along the clothes, she felt her suspicions grow. "Quite the fashion plate, aren't you, Avery?" she whispered, reaching into one of the suits to find the inside pocket so that she could read the label.

"Hugo Boss," she murmured, then checked another. "Armani. Apparently being a personal trainer pays really well."

The collection of designer duds was interesting, but it didn't tell her much about the man. Leaving the closet light on, she turned her attention to the dresser. She had just opened the third drawer when she heard a sound behind her.

Spinning, she found Avery lounging in the doorway.

"I—I can explain," she stammered, cursing herself for leaving the door unlocked.

"You bet you will."

Charly slammed the drawer closed, trying to buy time to think. Avery came into the room, closed the door, then casually reclined across the bed.

She probably wouldn't have been so nervous if he hadn't looked so calm. Damn him!

"I was looking for you," she said.

One brow arched suspiciously. "Behind a locked door?"

"I picked the lock because...I was concerned that you might have fallen in the shower."

"I see," he said with a nod. "And when I wasn't in the shower, you decided to look for me in the dresser drawer?"

Charly allowed her hands to fall to her sides. "I confess, Avery. I originally came here to see if you wanted to watch a movie with me."

"What movie?"

"What?"

He rose slowly. "What movie did you want me to watch with you?"

"I...*A Star Is Born.*"

He smiled down at her. "Janet Gaynor and Fredric March or the 1954 musical version with Garland and Mason?"

"Jan—Janet Gaynor," she stammered.

"Sounds great. Is there popcorn?"

CHAPTER SIX

"I'M DYING!"

"Ten more," Avery said. He loomed above her, spotting her on the weight-lifting apparatus.

"I can't!"

An exaggerated frown creased his brow. "You have to work off all that butter you put on the popcorn last night."

Straining, Charly favored her right arm as she pushed the weight on the bar toward the glare of the tack room's overhead light. "If you aren't going to put butter on popcorn, you might as well just eat cardboard."

He chuckled. "You have the worst eating habits of any person I've ever known."

"So?" Charly grunted, pulling herself into a sitting position on the weight bench. Perspiration trickled down her face and she blotted it with the towel he offered. Thanks to her rigorous workout, she had aches in muscles she hadn't known existed before.

"I can only conclude that good genes are responsible for your great body," Marshall went on. "But that's only the outside. Do you have any idea what all that fat and sugar is doing to your arteries?"

Charly tossed her towel at him. "Lighten up, Avery. I will never eat the way you do."

"You should."

"Food is a necessary pleasure for me. Besides, I'm a good ol' Southern belle, sugar. If it ain't fried, it ain't done."

"If you keep stuffing yourself with junk food and lounging on the couch watching videos, your body will give out before you're eligible for social security."

She battled the childish urge to stick out her tongue at him. "I'll worry about that when I'm older." She paused and offered a sweet smile. "Like you."

"I'm not old," he said.

Charly pulled a T-shirt over her spandex outfit. "I don't know Avery. By my calculations, you're dangerously close to the age when a man is required to sit on a bench in the middle of some mall while his wife shops."

"I don't have a wife."

"No plans to marry that woman you met near the pool house last night?"

For once Avery wasn't able to mask his surprise. He studied her quietly for a minute. "That was nothing."

Charly hated the sudden burst of elation she had no business feeling. The man had kissed her only because she had all but insisted. He was way out of her league and it would serve her well to remember as much.

"Am I dismissed?"

"I was thinking that some yoga might help you calm down. How long do you think you can last, catching a few hours of sleep here and there?"

Moving to the window, Charly looked out at the exercise pen where her sister Jax and Robert Bearclaw were working a new horse. As usual, Bear was communicating with the animal by placing his weathered face near the animal's ear. His long silver ponytail danced on the breeze as he tried to coax the horse into accepting a bit.

"Who's he?"

"Bear is our resident horse expert."

"I thought that was your sister."

"Jax learned everything from Bear. He put all of us in a saddle and taught us to ride."

"Are you any good?"

Tilting her head, she gave him a sidelong glance. "I'm exceptional."

She sensed Avery moving behind her. The feel of his body pressed against hers couldn't possibly be as incredible as the rush of anticipation she got just thinking about it. The thin T-shirt and second skin of spandex all but evaporated once she felt the heat of his closeness.

"I need to take a shower."

"I'd be happy to help."

Charly drew in a fortifying breath. "Is that how you got that closet full of designer clothes?" She turned around and lifted her face to look up at him. His warm breath washed over her but she didn't blink. "You wash my back and I buy you trinkets? Is that how this is supposed to work?"

His expression was stony, his eyes as black as night. "Everything I have, I earned."

"I'm sure," she said, stepping away. "Look, Avery,

I'm not your conscience or your mother, so you don't have to explain yourself to me.''

"Gee, thanks.''

"But please stop coming on to me.''

Avery moved quickly and quietly, blocking her exit with his massive body. His normally placid face was so hard and unyielding that a shiver of alarm inched along her spine. "I haven't come on to you.''

"Right,'' Charly replied with more bravado than she actually felt. "I guess I shared that mind-numbing kiss with some other personal trainer yesterday. My mistake.''

His expression softened and the corners of his mouth curled in a lecherous smile. "Mind-numbing, huh?''

Charly would have given anything for the floor of the tack room to open and swallow her whole. "Figure of speech.''

"Wanna bet?''

He moved toward her and she instinctively backed up until she could retreat no farther. Flattening his palms against the wall on either side of her head, Avery brought his face a mere fraction of an inch from hers.

"If you're going to kiss me to try to make some juvenile point, go ahead.''

"I was going to,'' he said, settling his lips just above hers. She smelled earthy and sexy. Charly stared at him with molten gray eyes. The only problem was, he didn't know if the emotion churning in them was fury or desire. He could handle a woman's desire, but he had never once touched a woman in anger. Before he humiliated himself, he latched tight on to his self-control. Without that control, he probably could have hauled her into his arms to explore the violent passion she so effortlessly incited in him.

His reaction to this woman didn't make sense and could get him into a heap of trouble. He had to remember that Charly was a job. It was just that she was such a contradiction, a very intriguing one. She was determined to be a great cop. She came from a wealthy family but didn't seem to put much stock in her cushy life-style. Seeing her apartment had told him that much. Even in its torn-apart status, he could see that it had been simply, inexpensively furnished. Seeing her lingerie had taken his mind in a completely different direction. Why was she so afraid of being a woman? And why did he notice little else? Charly was off-limits. But she was also the sexiest woman he had ever met.

Stepping back, he nodded his head in the direction of the door. "You'd best go up to the house and get in the shower, Charly. I'm taking you to meet with Agent Canfield of the FBI. He's at the federal building between here and New Orleans."

She walked away from him with the grace and elegance of a prima ballerina. At the door, she stopped but didn't turn around. "You don't have to take me."

"Either I come along or I tell your family about the calls."

"Why?"

"Ever consider the possibility that I'm just a nice guy?"

"Not really."

No kidding, he thought a half hour later as he buttoned his shirt and stuffed it into the waistband of his jeans.

"She's too observant," he said aloud, running a comb through his hair. "Too suspicious. And definitely too desirable."

Quietly, he made his way down the staircase, still bothered by his uncharacteristic lack of focus. *How can a five-foot-tall, hundred-pound woman do this to me?*

From the sound of muffled voices, he guessed Charly was in the kitchen.

"Do something with yourself, for heaven's sake. I swear, kiddo, it's like you to go out of your way to look horrid."

"Thanks, Marie. Don't you have anything better to do than drive out to Riverwood to give me a fashion critique for lunch?"

Avery moved into the shadows and peered at the two women through a crack in the door. If it weren't for their physical similarities, he would never have imagined the two women came from the same family. Their styles were dramatically different. Marie was exotic and flamboyant, a swirl of brightly colored fabric and jangling jewelry.

Charly's innate cynicism was the only thing standing between her and the label "fresh off the farm." Her skin had that just-scrubbed glow and sun-kissed blush. At first glance, the cutoff shorts and casual T-shirts gave her an air of innocence that made him feel protective. But he knew all too well that one look into those long-lashed, sultry gray eyes and the emotions she evoked were the furthest thing from innocent.

"I'm just trying to help," Marie said. "You have a gorgeous man running around and you don't even bother to put on makeup."

Charly flipped a chocolate candy into her mouth. "I wore lipstick last Saturday at the wedding."

"But, Charly, you have the perfect opportunity here. Marshall *is* a captive audience."

Charly downed a handful of candies. "Ever since you married Lucas, you've lost your perspective on male-female relationships. Before you met him, you wouldn't have even suggested that I look twice at a man like Avery."

"What is that supposed to mean?" Marie demanded.

"Look at him!" Charly fairly shouted. "Then look at me. Even if I was willing to paint my face and wear hooker heels, I'm not stupid enough to go after a man I know nothing about."

"Daddy hired him," Marie argued as she snatched the open bag of candy out of Charly's grasp. "Daddy would never bring a man into this house if he wasn't completely confident of his credentials."

"Daddy hasn't seen his closet," Charly grumbled.

"You *didn't!*" Marie wailed.

"I just took a quick look."

Marie balled her fist and rested it against her forehead. "When are you going to stop picking locks, Charly? It was cute when you were ten, but you aren't ten anymore."

"If I hadn't taught you how to pick locks, that crazy guy would have killed you and Lucas."

Avery made a mental note to ask about the crazy guy. Maybe he was still loose and had access to a phone.

"You can't equate the two," Marie argued. Then her voice softened. "So, what did you find in his closet?"

"Clothes."

"Clothes? In his closet? Hurry, dial 911."

"Funny," Charly replied. "Expensive clothes. Chameleon clothes."

"Like a costume? How kinky."

Charly shook her head. "Western wear, tailored suits... It's as if he's got the clothes to dress for any occasion, for any role."

"You are jaded, kiddo. Did you ever think that the guy just has eclectic taste?"

"No," she admitted. "I've been too busy wondering how a personal trainer can afford thousand-dollar loafers and a four-thousand-dollar watch."

"Maybe he has family money."

"Maybe," Marshall heard Charly grudgingly admit before he stepped into the room.

Marie's smile was genuine as she rose and handed him the bag of candy. "If she behaves, give her one."

"Cute, Marie."

"I almost forgot," Marie said, her bracelet-ladened arm reaching toward the door. "Beau told me to tell you that he and Dad have a meeting tonight, so I guess it will be just the two of you for dinner. Bye."

"I hope she gets postpubescent acne," Charly grumbled.

She stood, slipping her feet into sandals that looked worn and comfortable. When she bent down to retrieve her purse, Marshall stifled a groan. Those shorts should have been illegal, or at the very least come with an explicit warning.

"I want to leave Odelle a note," she said. "There's

no point in her cooking for just two. We can grab a burger on the way back. Or don't you do burgers?''

"I'll manage," he said.

He followed her to his truck, willing his mind back to the task at hand. He had to get his thoughts back on track. He had a job to do.

Charly climbed up into his truck without assistance, though she bit the inside of her cheek to keep from crying out. Her leg muscles felt as if they were on fire from all the unaccustomed exercise.

"Who is Agent Canfield?" she asked.

"He's the guy I talked to after the bomb went off. He seemed decent enough."

She adjusted the air-conditioning vent so that a steady stream of cool air hit her face and neck. "Does he know why I'm coming to see him?"

"Yep."

"Does he know not to say anything to my family?"

"I thought I'd let you handle the instructions."

Charly fell silent for a few minutes. "Are you mad about something?"

"Nope."

She regarded his profile. His jaw seemed taut, his mouth little more than a thin line. "You seem miffed about something."

His hands tightened on the wheel. "Why would I be miffed? You basically accused me of being some sort of money-sucking leech where women are concerned. I'm just having a hard time understanding what I've said or done to you to give you such a low opinion of me."

Charly rubbed her hands over her face. "Have you been taking lessons from my father?"

"Lessons in what?"

"In making me feel guilty."

He cast her a quick glance. "Do you feel guilty?"

"I shouldn't."

"Do you?"

She let out her breath slowly. "A little."

"Good."

She looked up to find him grinning. "I'm suffering guilt and that makes you happy?"

"No. I would just like to know that you're willing to give me the benefit of the doubt."

"That would be a tad easier if you would tell me something about yourself."

It was Avery's turn to let out a deep breath. "Like what?"

"We can start with the basics. Age, place of birth."

"I'm thirty-seven. I'm originally from Oklahoma."

"How long did 'originally' last?"

"High school."

"Then where?"

He appeared to concentrate on the street signs. "College, a stint in the military, then I sort of traveled around from place to place."

"As a personal trainer?"

"No."

"Okay, then, were you traveling around for business or pleasure?"

"A little of both."

"You're getting evasive and I haven't even gotten to the tough questions yet."

"If I tell you any more, I'll have to kill you," he said, then brandished that smile like a lethal weapon.

She could almost see a protective shield go up between them. If they hadn't reached the federal building, she would have pressed him further. At least she had gotten some useful information.

Charly and Avery passed through the security checkpoint, then took the elevator to the third floor. As they approached the receptionist's desk, she felt his fingers splay at the small of her back.

Her skin warmed, her heart skipped. How could such an innocent gesture have so powerful an effect on her?

I don't get all weird when a man touches me, she reminded herself. But Avery wasn't a man, he was more like an omniscient presence. It was driving her crazy. She'd worked too hard at putting her personal life on the back burner to allow anything to happen. Hormone rush or not, she couldn't afford to let schoolgirl reactions to a man dissuade her now. Not when she was so close to getting back to work.

A tall man in a dark suit, white shirt and striped tie emerged from one of the closed doors. Pushing his wire-rimmed glasses up the bridge of his nose, he extended his hand.

"You must be Miss Delacroix."

"Officer Charlotte Delacroix," she corrected him smoothly. "My friends call me Charly."

"I'm Agent Canfield."

"His friends call him Agent," Avery whispered in her ear as they followed the rather stiff man through the door and down a corridor.

"We can use this room," Canfield said, ushering

them into an area with a long wooden table and mis-
matched chairs. "I'll be right with you. Can I get you
anything? Coffee, a soft drink?"

"Coffee, three sugars," Charly answered, ignoring
Avery's pointed stare.

"Bottled water for me."

"Boring," Charly said in a stage whisper.

She pulled out a chair and sat, dropping her purse to
the floor and glancing around the austere surroundings.
The walls were empty except for a poster on child
safety, and the room was heavy with the scent of cherry
air freshener.

Agent Canfield returned, flanked by a harried-
looking woman carrying two disposable cups and a
bottle of water tucked beneath her arm. "Thank you,"
Canfield said as he placed two thick file folders on the
table, then relieved his employee of the beverages.
"Are you sitting in on this, Mr. Avery?"

The two men seemed to lock eyes briefly before
Avery said, "I'm a friend of the family. But I'll leave
if Charly wants to speak with you alone. Charly?"

She shrugged. "Stay if you want."

Avery turned one of the chairs around, then swung
his powerful thigh over the seat, settling into the chair
as if it were a saddle.

Canfield flipped open one of the files and scanned a
document while Charly took her first sip of the worst
coffee she had ever tasted.

When the agent looked up, he must have realized the
problem. "You get used to it after a while," he said.
He glanced back at the papers in front of him. "You
have a very…interesting family."

"Good adjective," she said with a smile.

"Marie Henderson is your sister?" he asked after another quick review of his file.

"Yes."

"She was indicted on murder charges last December?"

Charly bristled. "She was cleared when the real murderer tried to kill her and her husband."

Canfield had the decency to blush. "And Nikki Gideon, she's also a relative?"

"Nikki is a cousin. And she was also cleared of any involvement in the murder of Steven Boudreaux." Charly shoved the rancid coffee aside and leaned forward. "I just recently learned that my great-grandfather lost a murder case in 1938 and that my grandfather testified at the trial. Don't you want to add that to your little dossier?"

"I'm investigating a bombing, Charly. You should understand that I have to ask these questions."

She wasn't impressed. "I don't have a problem with your investigation, just the way you phrased your question. Marie's very brave actions saved the lives of her husband and an NOPD officer."

"Duly noted," Canfield replied. "Perhaps we should just move on."

"Good idea," Avery said, his hand reaching over to knead the tense muscles of her neck.

The action was oddly calming. "I've been getting anonymous phone calls since January," she told Canfield.

"Seven months?"

Charly nodded. "The calls started when I was in the

hospital recovering from a shooting. At first the caller would just hang up. Then, about a month ago, the guy started to talk.''

"The subject is male?''

"I think so.''

"It sounded like a man to me, too,'' Avery added.

"Can you remember what he said?''

Charly shivered. "He has decided it's time for me to die. But it sounds worse than it is,'' she insisted.

Canfield shuffled some of his papers. "Now, the shooting you referred to would be the incident at Swampy's Bar and Grill, right?''

"Yes.''

"Officer Frank Weatherspoon was fatally injured in the incident?''

"Yes.''

"You received a shoulder wound and a head wound?''

"Yes.''

"There are no suspects at this time?''

"Not that I know of,'' she said.

"You weren't able to provide sufficient information to effect an arrest?''

Charly glared at the man. "I never saw the shooter.''

Canfield nodded. "The calls began immediately thereafter?''

"I didn't answer the phone while I was in a coma, so I can only tell you that the first call I received was when I was moved to a private room about three weeks after the shooting.''

The agent eyed her as he twirled his pen with his

fingers. "There's no need for sarcasm. You have no idea who is making these calls?"

Charly looked over at Avery, who gave her a supportive nod. "It might be one of the officers in my department."

"Why do you think that?"

Suddenly restless, Charly rose and paced in the small area behind the chairs. "I'm the only woman ever to be hired on with the Slidell PD. Even though I had been a civilian employee of the New Orleans PD for more than a year, the guys all treated me like I was inferior. When Frank was killed, they decided I must have choked. That I didn't do everything possible to save his life."

"Did you?"

Charly rubbed her bare arms. "I don't know. I can't remember the shooting."

"Nothing at all?"

Charly fixed her eyes on a minute tear in a poster on the wall. "I have nightmares, but I still don't have a clear sense of what happened."

"Have you considered sleeping pills?" Canfield asked.

"Not after my hospital stay."

"Why?" The question came from Avery.

Charly waved her hand. "It was nothing. I had a major reaction to one of the medications they gave me in the hospital."

"Let's back up a bit," Canfield suggested. "What were your responsibilities with the New Orleans PD?"

"I was a computer programmer and analyst for the NOPD when I was at the academy. Computers were my minor in college. Mostly, I did routine stuff, database work and that sort of thing.''

"Tell him about Tesconti," Avery prompted.

Agent Canfield's head shot up at the mention of the crime boss's name.

"I designed the computer tracking system that the organized crime unit used when they were trying to build their case against Rico Tesconti," she explained.

Canfield pulled out a clean sheet of paper and looked as excited as a kid at a circus. "We are talking about *the* Rico Tesconti, right?"

"New Orleans by way of Brooklyn. Came here to work drugs, prostitution and to get his hooks into legal gambling to launder his money.''

"The indictment was quashed, right?''

Charly nodded. "No one went near the D.A. for a month. Apparently Tesconti is too high up and too protected.''

"Did any of his people know that you worked on the indictment?''

"Got me," Charly explained. "I was a lowly computer operator.''

"What about the officer who was killed? Did he work on the Tesconti case?''

"No," Charly answered quickly. "At least, he never said anything when I mentioned it to him.''

Canfield's forehead furrowed in a series of deep lines. "What things did you and your partner work on?''

"Nothing, really." Charly returned to the table and began scratching her initials into the side of her coffee cup. "I did an arrest on a guy for drunk driving. Frank did the other five because I don't speak Spanish and he did.''

"Spanish?''

"Yes, they were day pickers who probably spent their nights drinking. We also attempted to serve a warrant on a guy, but it didn't pan out. That is the sum total of my career to date.''

There was a knock on the door, and a woman summoned Canfield from the room. He returned a minute later and Charly noted that he no longer made eye contact.

"What about the bomb that was placed in your car?''

Charly shrugged. "I always leave my top down, so I guess it was an easy mark. I thought it was a wedding gift I was supposed to deliver.''

"Do you believe in coincidence, Charly?'' the agent queried.

"Not really.''

"And all these...events in your life aren't bothersome to you?''

"I really believe the calls are meant to scare me off.''

"What about the break-in at your apartment?''

"I haven't lived there for almost five months,'' Charly explained. "If someone really wanted to hurt me, they would come after me in Bayou Beltane.''

Canfield leaned back in his chair. "Who knows where you've been staying?''

"I haven't exactly been in hiding,'' she told him.

"Could you be more specific?''

"My family.''

"That includes half the parish," Avery grumbled as he stood up. "I'll be right back."

"Who else?" Canfield asked, once Avery had closed the door.

"Chief Harrington and anyone he might have talked to. Jada Crowley and anyone she might have talked to."

"The same Crowley who was at the wedding?"

Charly nodded. "We're good friends."

The conversation stopped when Avery slipped back into the room wearing an apologetic smile. "Sorry, I had to make a call."

"This Jada Crowley," the agent went on. "Is she the same Crowley who was involved in that mess a few years back?"

Charly bristled again, and Marshall knew that if she had been physically capable of spitting fire, Canfield would be toast.

"'Mess' is an interesting euphemism for date rape," she informed him in clipped syllables. "But yes, that was Jada."

"You testified on her behalf, didn't you?"

"Yes."

"Mason Ranier walked, right?"

"Yes."

"He's a pretty powerful man," Canfield acknowledged. "I hear he's thinking of running for Congress next time around."

Charly sneered. "I won't be voting for him."

"Have you had any contact with him since the trial?"

"Do you count the time, six months ago, when I screamed 'slimeball' at him in a movie theater?"

Avery chuckled with appreciation while Canfield pinched the bridge of his nose. After letting out a slow breath, the agent said, "For such a young woman, you sure do have an impressive list of potential enemies. I'll get on this right away, talk to your family, friends...."

Panic welled inside her. "You can't do that!"

"Why not?"

"My family will go ballistic if they think anything is wrong. My great-uncle Philip is always claiming to be five minutes away from death. My great-aunt Mary is recovering from a massive coronary, and Daddy doesn't need any more stress in his life."

"You've told me some very troubling things, Charly. You don't expect me to sit on my hands, do you?"

"Talk to Tesconti," she suggested. "But leave my family and friends out of this. Please?"

"You're not making this easy," Canfield warned.

Avery grasped her arm and gently tugged her to her feet. "Nothing about Charly is easy," he said, offering the man his hand. "We'll be in touch."

"This was a bad idea," she said, once they were back at the truck.

"Maybe," he responded absently, sliding behind the wheel. "Canfield sure does have your family history down pat."

"The revisionist version," she muttered. "Where are we going?"

"To dinner."

"I'm not hungry."

"Woman can't live on candy and coffee alone."

"This woman can. Really, Avery. Let's just go home."

"Not yet. We'll go into New Orleans and walk around. You'll work up an appetite."

"Goody," she grumbled, massaging her already aching thighs. "More exercise. Just what I need."

"You complain too much."

"So you've said."

He parked in a garage near the Central Business District, and after some cajoling, Charly stepped down from the truck, resigned to her fate.

New Orleans's streets were thick with tourists and street performers. They headed toward the Quarter at a leisurely pace.

"Did you like growing up here?" He slipped her hand into his as he finished the question.

"While it lasted." Catching their reflection in a shop window, Charly yanked her hand free.

"Why did you do that?"

She removed her sunglasses and shoved them into her purse. "If you hold my hand, people will think we're together."

"We are together."

"*Together* together."

He grasped her around the waist and swung her into the shadows of a nearby alley. Her skin tingled where his warm breath washed over her face. "I don't usually care what people think," he said in a hoarse whisper. "But I'm willing to make an exception in this case."

She tried to concentrate on verbalizing an appropriate put-down, but that was impossible. He assailed every cell in her body just by being near her. Her throat grew taut and dry as his eyes gently caressed her up-turned face.

His hands traveled to her shoulders and his thumbs slipped beneath the top of her T-shirt to skim across the tender flesh at the base of her throat. With one hand, he raked his fingers through her hair, gently applying just enough pressure to ease her head back.

Her own hands found their way to his chest, and she felt his heartbeat, fast and uneven, beneath the thin fabric. His mouth hovered dangerously close to hers, and he teased her with the promise of his kiss, feathering his lips against hers in a not-so-subtle hint of what was to come.

She knew she should stop this lunacy, but she didn't want to. She wanted more. Standing on tiptoe, she tried desperately to force the kiss. Avery countered the move, keeping his lips nothing more than a whisper against hers. With her palms, Charly explored the hardened muscles of his chest, tracing the outline of his nipples through his shirt.

When a low moan escaped him, Charly felt a sort of heady, feminine power. Then his arms locked around her, crushing her against him, and his mouth came down hard on hers. She pressed herself to him, unable to get close enough as he worked a special magic with his tongue.

He deftly explored the seam of her lips, before delving deeply into the welcoming interior of her mouth. Her knees threatened to buckle under the intensity of his kiss, and with a moan, Charly crushed her breasts against him, giving in to the overpowering passion that had invaded her.

And then it was over. Without warning, his hands stilled and he tore his mouth away, resting his forehead against hers. Neither one of them spoke. Not that she could have heard much over the sound of her own labored breathing. They stood like that for several seconds.

Charly wondered why she had all but attacked the man on a public street. When he gently set her away from him, she kept her eyes lowered. There was no point in adding insult to injury. No point in letting him see the hurt in her eyes, which was too raw to conceal.

"Charly," he began, and reached for her hand.

"Don't!" she snapped, slapping at him. "No post mortems. Let's just go home."

"Charly," he pleaded softly. "You've got me in an impossible position."

"We were pretty public," she agreed. She dug into her purse and retrieved her sunglasses. "I—"

"Even if we weren't in public," he reasoned softly, "this can't happen yet."

She blinked. "Yet?"

His eyes held regret. "Things are moving too fast between us," he said, and headed back to the noisy thoroughfare.

Charly stood watching him a minute, feelings of hurt and disappointment washing over her. Then her pride reasserted itself.

"*This* might just never happen, Marshall Too-Sure-of-Yourself Avery," she vowed, and stormed out of the alley after him.

CHAPTER SEVEN

"ODELLE! WE'RE BACK!" Charly called as they stepped into the darkened kitchen. As soon as she flipped on the light, she saw the note propped against the fruit bowl in the center of the table. "She left some chicken in the fridge," Charly said after reading the note.

Dropping her purse on the table, she grabbed the step stool and dragged it behind her. Avery moved swiftly, placing himself between her and the cabinet above the stove.

Remembering how easily she had melted in his arms, she didn't dare make contact.

"You're going to have a real meal. You've hardly eaten all day."

She opened her mouth to protest, then, seeing the determined set of his jaw, sighed with resignation.

"Go sit. I'll cook."

"Does this mean I have to clean up?" she asked. The best course was to keep their conversation light and harmless.

"You bet."

"Then nuke everything so I'll only have to wash plates."

She had an unobstructed view of his incredible rear

end as he rummaged in the refrigerator. Light and harmless was getting more difficult by the second.

"How does salad with chicken and vinaigrette sound?"

"Like it will be heavy on the salad and light on the chicken."

He cast her a sidelong glance. "Be nice or I'll make you help."

"I won't say another word," she promised as she reached for the neat stack of mail. "Are we allowed to have wine with our meal, or is alcohol on your long list of sins?"

"My sin list is pretty short, but you're at the top."

"You're a hopeless flirt," she grumbled, before selecting a bottle of wine from the pantry.

Avery was busy slicing and dicing various greens and vegetables, which allowed Charly an opportunity to study him. He seemed equally at home in the kitchen as he did in the workout room. The man was a mass of contradictions, and he intrigued her.

"You're quiet."

"Mmm," she murmured, taking a sip of the wine she had poured. "Where did you learn to cook?"

He lifted his broad shoulders. "I picked it up here and there. I had to learn to cook or else spend the rest of my days eating at restaurants."

"Where is here and there?"

Avery scraped up some cucumber and transferred it to the side of the cutting board. "I pulled a lot of KP during my military career."

"Sounds like punishment."

He smiled. "It was. I wasn't very good at respecting authority in those days."

"And you're better at it now?"

He gave her a sheepish look. "Sometimes."

Charly tried to imagine him in a uniform. He would look wonderful in just about anything, but she was finding it difficult to imagine independent, opinionated Avery taking orders from anyone.

"Were you going to make the military a career?"

"I never really gave it any thought." He went to the refrigerator and made a production out of selecting two chicken breasts.

"All the taste is lost if you take the skin off," Charly said.

"It also doesn't have all that fat."

"No fat, no flavor," she said.

He cast her a quick glance. "Has anyone ever told you that you are a nutritionist's worst nightmare?"

"Just my entire family and Jada."

"Jada?"

Charly took another sip of wine. The alcohol was beginning to mask the tension that seemed to be her constant companion these days. "Jada 'got religion' about food a few years ago. I don't care what the experts say, I'd rather eat Moon Pies than tofu any day."

His laughter filled the kitchen. It was a rich, deep, masculine sound that touched her like a caress. She wanted to believe it was just the wine. He crushed garlic and used a whisk to create a dressing. Muscle strained against the fabric of his shirt, drawing her eyes and sparking her fantasies. It was absolute lunacy. Avery was out of her league.

"Dinner is served," he said as he placed a huge bowl of freshly tossed salad in the center of the table.

Charly poured some wine into his glass, then topped off her own. She eyed the salad cautiously. "It looks...healthy."

Avery lifted a mound of the greens onto her plate. He did the same for himself, then took the seat next to her. Raising his glass, he said, "To healthy."

"To Moon Pies."

In spite of her avowed policy never to eat rabbit food, Charly ate with enthusiasm. She decided it had to be the wine.

"You didn't die," Avery joked when they had finished and he was carrying the plates to the sink.

"Wait till this stuff gets into my system." She stood up and moved to the sink, turning on the tap.

"This can wait." He reached across her to shut off the water. "I'd like to talk."

When his forearm brushed her rib cage, she wasn't sure she was capable of speech. She simply nodded and followed him back to the table.

"Tell me about the crazy man who went after your sister Marie."

Charly ran her fingertip around the rim of her wineglass. "Ken Rossner framed Marie for murder. When she and Lucas started to investigate on their own, he tried to kill them both."

"What happened to him?"

"Marie shot him. Why are you asking?"

Avery shrugged. "I'm trying to figure out who is behind all this."

Charly frowned. "Rossner is in jail. So tell me,

Avery, why does a personal trainer care about a break-in at my apartment?''

Cocking his head to the side, he flashed her a smile. "I like to think of myself as a full-service operation.''

Charly willed herself not to be distracted by the display of even white teeth, or the fact that his large hand now covered one of hers. Ignoring the tingle of excitement inching up her arm, she met his cool, dark stare. "You ask too many of the right questions.''

"I'm a bright guy,'' he explained easily.

"I'm sure you are.'' Charly pulled her hand away. "You sound like a cop.''

There was a flicker of something before he said, "Ex-cop, for Uncle Sam.''

Charly nodded. "That explains why you know just what to ask. It doesn't explain your interest.''

Averting his eyes, Avery took a long drink of his wine. "I guess I can't sit back while some sicko haunts a beautiful woman. My mother raised me better than that.''

Charly made a disgusted sound. "Try again.''

He reached out and captured her chin between his thumb and forefinger. Applying gentle pressure,. he lifted her chin until their eyes met. "Is your self-esteem really that low?''

"There's nothing wrong with my self-esteem.''

"Then tell me why you use your brother and your best friend like shields? Or why you use your caustic wit to keep people at arm's length?''

Charly jerked her head away, breaking his hold. "You're nuts, Avery. I'll bet you learned just enough psychology in college to be dangerous.''

He sighed heavily. "I know enough about human nature to recognize what's wrong with you."

She bristled. "There isn't anything wrong with me. Maybe I'm not at my best right now. Being shot and almost blown up will do that to a person."

"Okay, let's get back to that. For now."

Charly crossed her arms over her chest. "I'll agree that a whole lot of weird stuff has been happening, but I can't believe any of it is related."

"You're sure the guy who went after Marie is in jail?"

"Yep," Charly answered. "He was committed to a state hospital for the criminally insane."

"We can check on that." Avery reached behind him and grabbed a pen and paper from the counter. "Tell me about this Mason Ranier character."

Charly felt a shiver of revulsion dance along her spine. "He's a pig."

"You know that firsthand?"

"Mason is a rapist," Charly stated bluntly.

"I thought he was a politician."

"Are the two mutually exclusive?"

He smiled. "Point. But I didn't get the impression that you and Agent Canfield were speaking in the philosophical."

"Mason and Jada met when Jada was in grad school."

"It wasn't love at first sight?" he guessed.

"It was. At least for Jada. They dated for about six weeks when it happened."

"It?"

"Mason had been pressuring Jada for sex since their

first date. One night he decided he wouldn't take no for an answer. Jada pressed charges. The jury screwed her a second time.''

Avery took her hand in both of his. "So where did you fit in?"

His touch was soothing, as was the soft cadence of his voice. "I testified against him."

"I'm guessing he didn't thank you for that?"

Her laugh was void of humor. "During cross-examination, Mason's lawyer ripped me to shreds. After the trial, Mason himself said some pretty ugly things."

"What could his attorney possibly say to discredit you?"

She met his piercing gaze. "He implied that I had made an overture to Mason. He made it sound like the only reason I was testifying was because Mason had blown me off."

Avery grimaced. "Ouch."

"After that experience, the thought of becoming a lawyer, of becoming like him, turned my stomach."

Avery nodded with sudden realization. "So you decided to become a cop."

"Pretty noble, huh?"

"Understandable," he said. "How long ago did this happen?"

"Three years," she answered.

Avery dropped her hand to stroke the shadow of a beard on his chin. "Any reason why he might want to hurt you or Jada now?"

"He's about to announce his candidacy for Congress."

"But anyone who cared could get trial transcripts," Avery said.

Charly shook her head. "Jada's father pulled some strings and had the courtroom and the records sealed. The only thing that made it into the papers was Mason's arrest and his exoneration."

"Has he been in trouble since then?"

Charly shrugged. "I haven't exactly run my life around Mason Ranier's comings and goings."

"If he committed rape once," Avery cautioned, "chances are he will do it again."

"That's comforting," she mumbled. "But if Mason really wanted to hide his past, he would go after Jada, not me. Besides, Mason isn't man enough to harass me."

"Tesconti is."

"Assuming Tesconti had the first clue that I worked on the indictment."

"Can you find out whether he did?"

"I suppose I could call Detective Doucet at the NOPD and ask."

"Do that."

"WHERE ARE YOU GOING?" *Dressed like that,* he wanted to add. A slim denim skirt brushed the tops of her thighs, revealing a length of tanned, bare leg. He was unsure what to call her top, since there wasn't all that much of it. The thin, skin-tight swatch of red material left her shoulders and midriff exposed.

"Detective Doucet gave me the names of some places where I might find Tesconti."

"Whoa!" he said, grabbing her arm. "You're going

out at 11:00 p.m. to seek out one of New Orleans's biggest crime bosses?''

"That's the plan,'' she answered, jerking free.

"The plan just changed,'' he said firmly, and he pried the keys from her hand.

Charly glared up at him. "Don't be difficult, Avery. You're the one who suggested Tesconti might be behind all this. I believe in the direct approach.''

"The suicidal approach is more like it. Haven't you read the tourist brochures? It isn't safe for a woman alone at night.''

"I'm a woman *cop*,'' she reminded him as she made a futile attempt for the keys he held just out of her reach. "Don't be a pain.''

"Be smart, Charly.''

"Be quiet, Avery,'' she countered. "You aren't my keeper.''

"You sure as hell need one, darlin'.''

"I'm only going to talk to the man.''

Marshall swallowed his frustration. If he had learned anything about Charly, it was that she didn't respond well to authority. "Can I come along?''

She blinked at his suddenly conciliatory tone. "Come with me?''

"Yes.''

Her eyes narrowed. "Why?''

He let the keys dangle from his finger tauntingly. "I've never seen New Orleans at night.''

"I'm not going to the trendy spots,'' Charly warned. "And I doubt that anyone will talk to me if you tag along.''

"Either I come, or you don't go.''

Rolling her eyes, Charly gave him an impatient glare. "Have you been taking lessons from Beau?"

"I'm a quick study," he said. "Do we have a deal?"

"Suit yourself," Charly grudgingly agreed. "But I want you to stay out of my way."

"You won't even know I'm there," he promised.

Three hours later, he was following Charly into the seventh sleazy bar. This place was like so many other dives he'd seen over the years. Only the choice of music seemed to change.

As they moved up to the horseshoe-shaped bar, Marshall was aware that several pairs of eyes were on them. "Do you realize you're the only woman in here who isn't for sale by the hour?" he asked against her ear.

"Now who's being cynical?" she retorted, lifting herself onto a stool and crossing her legs. "I'll have whatever you've got on tap," she told the bartender.

A skinny man with several gaudy gold chains weighing down his wrist slid a napkin across the bar. Marshall felt his blood pressure rise a notch when the scrawny pig gave Charly a rather thorough once-over.

"Sure thing, sugar."

Marshall was ignored while the bartender went to the tap with a mug. He glanced around the room, taking in each face in turn. Scarred wooden tables were haphazardly arranged around a parquet dance floor, and less than a dozen patrons sat nursing drinks and negotiating with hookers.

The bartender returned and gave Charly her drink and a lecherous smile that revealed a chipped front tooth.

"Can I get you anything else, sugar?"

"Actually," Charly began, "I'm looking for a man."

"You've found him, sugar."

Marshall coiled like a snake, ready to strike if the bartender crossed the line.

"Actually, I'm trying to find a friend of a friend."

"I'm a friendly guy."

You're a regular purple dinosaur, Marshall thought with disgust.

"My friend's name is Rico," she said innocently. "Rico Tesconti. Know where I can find him?"

The bartender's eyes narrowed to little more than bluish slits. "Who's looking for him?"

"Me. I'm Charly."

The bartender spared Marshall a glance. "What about him?"

Charly didn't even flinch. "He's my...personal assistant."

The bartender seemed to relax. "Finish your beer, I'll see what I can do."

"Personal assistant?" Marshall whispered.

"I couldn't think of anything better. I knew I should have left you back in Bayou Beltane."

He picked up her beer and took a long swallow. "You really think you could hold your own in a place like this?"

"I do know how to handle myself," she hissed.

"Ever been in the middle of a barroom brawl?"

"No."

Marshall turned and rested his elbows on the bar. "I have, and I'll tell you, it isn't pretty."

"You're exaggerating."

He held his hair away from his ear. "See that scar?"

"Yes."

"That's what a bottle of Scotch whiskey does."

"When and where did you get that?"

"A few years back in a fight outside a bar in London."

"England?"

"No, China," he said with a playful wink. "What do you think is taking that bartender so long?"

"I don't know and I don't much care. I just hope he knows more than the dozen of others we've talked to tonight."

"Don't hold your breath."

Just then the man in question emerged from the back room. Marshall noted the thin line of perspiration on his forehead, and warning bells went off in his head.

"Sorry, sugar," he said, grabbing her half-full mug and pointedly dumping the contents into the sink. "Rico isn't around anymore."

"I see." Charly sighed. "Too bad, since I was willing to offer a finder's fee."

One black brow arched with interest. "A fee, huh?"

Charly reached into her purse and extracted several bills. At least she had the sense to shield the denomination. "Not a good idea to flash cash in this crowd," Marshall warned.

She brushed him off with a swat of her hand. "It's really important that I hook up with Rico."

"You heat?" the bartender queried.

"This is personal," she said, placing the bills on the

bar and covering them with her hand. Slowly, she slid them in the bartender's direction. He went for the bait.

"I guess I could make another call, sugar."

"Do that," Charly said. She lifted her hand and the bartender snatched up the cash.

"You'll regret that," Marshall warned.

She smiled smugly. "This is the Big Easy, baby. A city famous for graft, corruption and sin."

"And you're dressed for it."

"What is that supposed to mean?"

He allowed his eyes to roam boldly over her face, her throat, the swell of her breasts. Over the exposed flesh at her waist, over her slim skirt, then down her thighs, all the way to where her toes peeked out from her sandals. He was slow and deliberate, fully intent on illustrating his point. But his point got lost somewhere along the way. A simmer started in his gut, low and rumbling. The heat shifted to his loins, and he brought his hands up and placed them on her shoulders.

Her skin was warm and incredibly soft. He looked at her slightly parted lips. He could almost feel the catch of breath in her throat as his thumbs made circles against her bare flesh. It would be so easy to just dip his head and take her mouth. Easy, and a major mistake. He had to rein in—a difficult task when he saw the first hint of passion gleam in her sultry eyes.

His hands fell away just seconds before the bartender returned.

"Okay, sugar. Seems you're in luck."

"I doubt that." Marshall's snide comment earned him an elbow from Charly.

"I know a guy who knows a guy who is willing to talk to you."

"Good," Charly said.

Marshall reached across the bar and grabbed the man's tie. Wrapping it once around his fist, he jerked the little bozo until his eyes bulged in their sockets. "Not good enough," he warned.

"Let him alone!" Charly yelled.

Ignoring the four or five drunks who had stumbled to their feet, possibly with the grand notion of mounting a rescue, Marshall turned and gave silent challenge with his eyes. No one else moved.

The bartender sputtered and coughed. "I can't do any better than this. I swear!"

"You won't have a jaw left to swear with if you're jerking the lady around."

"I'm not," he insisted. "The lady should go to the alley off Rue de la Guerre in twenty minutes. Danny will meet her there."

Marshall gave the little twerp a shove as he released him. "An alley?"

Charly grabbed his arm. "I know where it is. We'll be fine there."

Marshall allowed himself to be dragged from the bar. When they stepped out into the early morning air, he took a deep, much-needed breath.

"You could have blown it, Avery," Charly stormed as she marched toward the lot where they had left her car. "If you have, I'll kick you. I didn't come all the way down here, trudging from one sleazy bar to another, just to have you ruin everything by flexing your testosterone."

"Get real, Charly. That guy played you like a guitar."

"That guy," she argued, "has been a bag carrier for Tesconti for years."

"Then why did it take him two calls to set up a meet?"

Charly spun around to say something else and they nearly collided. Instinctively, Marshall reached out and steadied her at the entrance to the lot. It should have been a simple act of politeness. He shouldn't have noticed that her legs were against his. Or that her oval face was tilted expectantly upward.

But he did notice, and he reacted. Tossing aside the recriminations that leapt to his mind, he pulled her into a crushing embrace. He wanted to feel every inch of her. He wanted to satisfy his perverse need for this woman once and for all. His reaction to her was clouding his judgment.

His mouth covered hers hungrily. He saw a burst of light, and for a split second credited Charly's unexplainable power over him. He lifted his head at the same instant that his legs buckled. Charly's scream was the last thing he heard before falling into a dark abyss.

CHAPTER EIGHT

"WAKE UP!" SHE DEMANDED, struggling against the ropes that tied them together. Since they had been tied back to back, she had no way of knowing exactly why Avery hadn't moved in the thirty or so minutes since their captors had left. She hoped he was just unconscious. She tried calling again. "Avery!"

He moaned and she felt a surge of hope.

"Avery! Come on, wake up!"

"I'm up," he said hoarsely. "Where exactly is up?"

"An old cannery out by Fletcher's Wharf."

"How'd you figure that out?" he remarked dryly.

"They blindfolded me in the car, but I could still see a bit. I know how long we were on the road, and I also recognized some of the graffiti on the side of the building."

"You're a regular Boy Scout."

"Too bad you weren't. Boy Scouts are good with knots." She punctuated her remark by straining against the ropes.

"I am prepared," he said. "There's a knife in my left front pocket. See if you can get it."

Charly wriggled and twisted until she managed to get her hand in his pocket. "I've got it."

"Uh, Charly?"

"Yes?"

"That isn't the knife."

She grimaced and jerked her hand in another direction. Maybe it was good that they were tied up in such a way that Avery couldn't see her face. She was blushing all the way to the roots of her hair. "Is that it?"

"Yes. Though it was more fun when you were wrong."

"One more crack like that and I'll cut your tongue out."

"Sorry. Pass me the knife and I'll cut the ropes."

"I can do it."

"Have you ever used a switchblade before?"

"No."

"Then give it to me, please. I'd like to leave here with only a skull fracture."

She flinched as his meaning struck her. "I'm sorry. How are you feeling?"

"I'll live."

The ropes fell away, and Avery grasped her hand at the very instant the door opened.

Charly was blinded by the beam of the flashlight until Avery tucked her safely behind him.

The sound of guttural laughter ricocheted off the walls. "I see you've made good use of your time here. Well done."

Avery kept one hand on Charly while the other went to the back of his head. "I wish you'd been as jovial when your goons were smashing my brains."

A trio of well-dressed men came into the cannery, and Charly craned her neck around Avery so she could see them better.

"I hope you will forgive that minor misunderstanding, Mr. Avery."

"Should I, Mr. Tesconti?"

"A simple matter of miscommunication. I had no idea that the woman looking for me was Charlotte Delacroix."

Charly slipped out from behind Avery, who insisted on keeping a tight hold around her waist. The beam from the flashlight now bounced off the floor, casting an eerie shadow across the gangster and his two flunkies.

Tesconti looked every bit the crime boss he was, from his expensive suit to the flashy rings on his fingers. His silver hair was styled so neatly it looked like a wig, and the raincoat draped over his shoulders gave him a regal air.

"Nice to meet you, Officer Delacroix," he said, and reached for her hand.

Charly was speechless as the dapper-looking gentleman lifted her hand to his lips, brushing a kiss across her knuckles. It should have made her skin crawl, but it didn't. Tesconti had more charm in his little finger than most men had in their whole body. No wonder indictments didn't stick.

"Please allow me to give you a ride back to your car."

"Sure," Avery said.

Charly and Avery walked with Tesconti while the two lackeys followed mutely behind.

A long, shiny limousine was parked and waiting beneath a street lamp. As they neared the vehicle, another man slipped from the shadows and held the door open.

Tesconti took her hand once more as she stepped into the posh interior. Running lights revealed an entertainment center, a wet bar and a bank of telephones. The letter *T* was sewn into the carpet and repeated on the curtains covering the windows.

Avery eased in beside her, placing a proprietary hand on her knee. Tesconti joined them next, settling his big body against the soft leather seat. The scent of his cologne filled the small compartment as he tossed off his coat and reached to pour himself a drink.

Charly could tell by the sounds of footsteps and doors opening and closing that the others had piled into the front of the limo. She wasn't sure if that was good or bad.

Tesconti watched her with piercing blue eyes, then said, *"Salute,"* and tossed back a shot of amber liquid.

"Is there some reason that you had us kidnapped after Mr. Avery was brutally assaulted?" Charly swallowed the cry that came to her lips when Avery pinched her leg.

Tesconti offered an indulgent smile. "You live up to your reputation. I have heard you are…blunt."

Charly was dying to ask where he'd picked up that bit of info but restrained herself. "And you've lived up to yours," she said instead. "Kidnapping is illegal."

"Mr. Tesconti has already explained that," Avery injected with a pointed glare. "Isn't that right?"

"Quite right, Mr. Avery. Tell me, what is your connection to the Delacroix?"

"I'm just an employee."

Tesconti nodded slowly. "Since when does a Delacroix—"

"I'm Charly's personal trainer."

Tesconti studied Avery for a moment, then shrugged. "Was allowing her to seek me out part of your personal training?"

Charly sat forward. "Excuse me, Mr. Tesconti, but nobody *allows* me to do anything. Avery was just along for company."

"Is that so?"

"Yes," she assured him. "Now he can probably sue me for a work-related injury, thanks to your... employees. And why aren't we moving?"

Tesconti waved his hands in a dismissive gesture. "Mr. Avery won't sue. We aren't moving because I was under the impression that you wished to speak with me."

"Did you know that I worked on the records trace that was used against you last year?"

Tesconti grinned. "So this has something to do with that farce of a charge?"

"You tell me," Charly challenged. "I've been having a bit more than my share of trouble lately."

"I heard about the explosion at the wedding," Tesconti said, making the sign of the cross. "Marriage is a sacrament. What kind of animal would commit such a sin before God?"

"We'll make sure the bomber says several Hail Marys when we find him," Avery said.

"You come to me about this bomb?" Tesconti asked, shock evident on his contorted features. "What possible reason could I have for harming you or your family?"

"You tell me," Charly said.

"I can't, because there isn't one," Tesconti insisted. "I'm a businessman, Officer Delacroix. Blowing up the wedding of south Louisiana's premier family isn't good for business."

"Have any of your friends heard anything?" Avery asked.

"One is always hearing rumors, Mr. Avery."

"You think any of those rumors might interest Charly and me?"

Tesconti's demeanor grew solemn, almost menacing. "How do I know this isn't a setup?"

"You don't," Avery answered immediately.

The two men seemed to share a private moment. It irritated Charly to be treated like an afterthought. "*Do* you know anything?" she demanded.

Her question broke the spell.

"I haven't heard anything for several months, and even then, I wasn't sure the information was reliable."

"What information?" Charly pressed.

"There was some talk."

"Talk?"

Tesconti met her gaze. "There was some discussion about a professional being brought in to take care of a sensitive problem."

"What kind of sensitive problem?"

Tesconti shrugged. "I never knew, but the next day I heard you had been shot."

"WHAT'S THE HOLDUP?"

"That broad has more people around her than the damned mayor!"

"*That broad can hang us all!*"

"*Not me,*" he said, using the tip of his blade to clean his teeth. "*I'll take care of it.*"

"*When?*"

He could almost smell the fear over the phone. He liked that. Liked the power. "*I've got an idea.*"

"*Ideas won't solve the problem. I need action. I paid for action.*"

With a flick of his wrist, he buried the knife up to its hilt. The blade entered squarely between her eyes. Too bad it was just a photo. He was getting tired of hanging around, waiting. It was dangerous to stay in one place too long.

"*You'll get your money's worth,*" he insisted. "*But it has to be clean.*"

"*Like that screwup at the wedding? Now the whole parish is crawling with feds.*"

"*No one saw me,*" he insisted. "*No one can trace the bomb back to us.*"

"*Why did you go to that damned wedding? What if there's a picture of you? What if someone remembers you?*"

"*It won't happen. I'm invisible.*"

"*That attitude will fry us both. Why don't you just do like I said? Kill her and dump her body in the swamp. She won't be found for years. By then, no one can link her to me.*"

"*I have something a little more creative in mind for sweet little Charly.*"

"*Then get to it!*"

"THREE MORE," Avery said, ignoring her complaints of pain. "Stop yelling. I have a killer headache."

"You should have let Lucas take a look at your head."

"It's just a bump. I've had worse falling from a horse."

"You ride?" she grunted as she lifted the last, hated weight.

"Yep." He tossed her a towel. "After you shower and change your shirt, maybe you'd like to show me Bayou Beltane by horseback."

She smiled sweetly. "You don't like my shirt?" She held it out and reread the scripted message: Exercise Regularly, Die Anyway. "Do you think it's smart for you to be on a horse with that knot on your head?"

"I'm tougher than that," he promised. "I'll meet you at the stables in about an hour?"

"You bet," she agreed. Her eyes were still on the door long after Avery had left. It wasn't a date, she reminded herself. Still, her pulse was just a little faster than normal and it had nothing to do with the grueling morning workout he had put her through.

"By the time he's finished with me, I'll be able to leap tall buildings in a single bound," she whispered. Then, wincing, she amended, "Maybe it'll take more than one bound."

After a soak in the tub, Charly grudgingly admitted that she did feel a little stronger. If she kept up this pace, she could be back to work in no time.

Walking over to the closet, she grabbed her jeans and a cotton shirt. Once dressed, she toweled her hair, then combed it. She left her boots for last. "Ouch," she muttered when she put too much pressure on her bad arm. Frustration gripped her as she massaged the dull ache in her shoulder.

"Feeling sorry for yourself isn't productive," she admonished herself, then stepped back into the bathroom to get a barrette before heading downstairs.

She found Odelle in the kitchen, wrapping sandwiches in plastic.

"If your daddy or your brother were here, they would forbid this."

"Forbid what?" Charly asked, popping an olive into her mouth.

"You got no business on a horse."

Charly gave the housekeeper a hug. "We're just going out on the trails. I wasn't planning on dressage jumps. I thought I'd save that for tomorrow."

"I swear," Odelle muttered, "you will be the death of us all. Sometimes I wonder if you use the brains the good Lord gave you."

Charly sighed and breathed in the yeasty smell of bread baking. "Is that your famous sourdough loaf I smell?"

Odelle gave her a withering look and placed her hands on her hips. "You know it is, and don't try to change the subject."

Charly raised her hands in surrender. "I'm doing no such thing. I was just complimenting you."

"Complimenting, my foot," Odelle huffed. "You're just trying to sweet-talk me so that I won't tell your daddy what a fool thing you're doing."

"You won't tell him, anyway," Charly countered,

hugging the older woman. "Who are you making the sandwiches for?"

"You and that man."

Charly chuckled. "That man?"

Odelle snorted. "You know who I mean. There's something fishy about that one. You mark my words."

Charly swallowed. She knew full well that Odelle was a pretty astute judge of character. "He won't be here long."

"Don't I know it."

Charly frowned as the housekeeper filled a basket with enough food for an army. "You don't need to pack all that," Charly said. "Avery can probably live off the grass and berries in the swamp."

Odelle kept heaping food into the basket. "You never know. Maybe that lady friend of his has an appetite."

"What lady friend?"

"The one he's been meeting out by the pool house."

Charly raced to the window and pushed aside the curtains. "Where?" she asked, not wanting Odelle to know that she was only too aware of Avery's "lady friend."

Odelle sighed. "By the trees. She showed up about twenty minutes ago."

"You saw her?"

"'Course I did."

"And?"

"And what, Charly? I think it's despicable that the man brings his woman here at all hours of the day and night. Really, you'd think he'd have better breeding."

Charly's eyes darted around the pool, searching for them. "Do you know who she is?"

"That's obvious enough, isn't it?"

Charly dropped the curtain. "I guess."

"What kind of lines has that boy been using on you?"

"It isn't like that," she insisted. "Avery might flirt, but it's harmless."

"A man looks that fine, nothing he says or does is harmless. You keep your head with him, girl, y'hear?"

"My head is just fine," she said, picking up the picnic basket. *It's my libido that's in trouble.*

The sun was hiding behind thick clouds, which kept the air temperature bearable. Staying on the path, she walked past the cabin where Jax had lived until her recent marriage. Farther down, she passed Beau's cabin. A smile touched her lips as she recalled what Jada had told her a few months back. It seemed that in some parts of Bayou Beltane, Beau's cabin was known as the Love Shack.

"I hope that smile is for me."

Charly nearly jumped when Avery appeared at her side. "Sorry."

"I sense a sudden chill in the air."

"Nope." Charly kept walking.

"You made lunch?"

"Sure."

He started to reach for the basket, but she held it just out of his reach.

"What's in there?"

"Ring-Dings, Drakes cakes and Twinkies for dessert."

He laughed. "I should have guessed."

"Well, well," Bear said as he emerged from one of the paddocks. He wiped his brow with the back of his hand. "I was wondering how long it would be before you got the itch to ride."

Charly gave the older man a one-armed hug. He smelled of the outdoors. "It feels like it's been forever."

Bear's black eyes narrowed. "Are you sure you're up to this?"

"I'm only going to take Avery on a walking tour."

"And a romantic lunch at Blackhawk Landing?"

Charly felt her cheeks warm. "Marshall Avery is my personal trainer. I assumed you'd met."

Bear offered his hand. "Mr. Avery, sorry about that crack. I just assumed...well, she doesn't usually bring men down—"

"He gets the picture," Charly said. "I'm not up to saddling, so would you mind?"

"Sure thing." Bear turned to Avery. "How about you?"

"Carry on. I'll handle my own."

"Got any experience in the saddle?"

"Enough."

Charly waited at the entrance to the paddocks. She kept an eye out for Avery's mystery woman. Who was she? A companion? A fiancée? A lover? "Like it's any of my business," she muttered.

"All set?" Avery asked as he came up and took the picnic basket from her. He tethered it behind his saddle.

"Sure," she said, taking the reins from Bear. Slipping her foot into the stirrup, she hopped twice before swinging herself up onto the animal's back. Clicking her tongue, she turned the well-trained animal toward the gate where Bear now stood.

"You keep to the trail," he warned.

"We will. We'll be back in a few hours."

"Keep an eye on her, Avery!"

"Will do!" she heard him call.

Not far from Riverwood, forest and swamp seemed to meld together. The horse knew the terrain almost as well as Charly. Mist swirled off the muddy waters of the bayou, spinning around the gnarled trunks and branches and giving a surreal feeling to their surroundings.

"You'd never know anyone lived here," Avery said as he brought his horse up beside hers. "What's that sound?"

"Insects," she answered, "and a couple of frogs."

"What's the smell?"

"Swamp vegetation. You'll get used to it in a little while."

"It smells like it just rained," he mused. "Clean, renewed."

"Apparently fresh air makes you wax poetic."

"Apparently it makes you surly. What's the deal?"

"No deal."

Avery reached over and reined her horse along with his own. "Your eyelashes flutter when you lie."

"Really?" She didn't look at him.

"I thought we were friends, Charly. Has something happened? Did you get another call?"

"No." She sighed. *I'm just being a jerk. So the guy has a girlfriend. So what? Get a grip.* "I guess I'm just a little tired from our clandestine meeting with Tesconti."

Somewhat reluctantly, Avery relinquished control of her horse and they continued along the bank of the swamp. Charly dismounted when they reached a steep incline. "Grab the basket. We have to walk from here."

They tied the horses to a tree, and Charly led the way through the thick underbrush.

"Are you sure you know what you're doing?"

"I grew up here," she said. "I know this swamp inside out."

"I hope so." Avery's tone didn't convey a great deal of confidence.

"Low branches," she called.

After clearing the next gully, she led him to a spot where a pirogue sat at the edge of the river. "Isn't this beautiful," she whispered reverently as she looked out across the bayou at the lush forest that seemed to be guarding the murky water.

Without fear, she removed her boots, waded out and pulled the boat from the shore. "Get in," she said.

Joining Avery, she grabbed the push pole and guided the boat into the center of the water. Cypress and tupelo seemed alive, as if their branches were reaching for the water of their own volition.

"Want me to do that?" he asked.

Charly smiled at him. "Nope. I know every inch, every lily and every gator nest. It's a whole lot safer if you just relax and play tourist."

She turned and found him staring at her with intensity. "What?"

"I'm impressed and a little surprised."

For some reason, his unexpected compliment caused her heart to flutter. *Must be sleep deprivation.* "Surprised?"

"It would take a whole lot of coaxing before you could convince me to wade in this water. But it doesn't even faze you."

"My uncle Remy says that if you respect the bayou, it can't hurt you."

"Does Uncle Remy know what a snake is?"

Charly laughed just as a fish broke the surface of the water. "Yes. He runs a boat landing and spends every waking hour on the water. He's very familiar with the dangers of the swamp."

Avery stretched his big body. "I could learn to like this," he said, locking his fingers together and resting his head in their cradle. Filtered sunlight licked at his handsome features as he closed his eyes with a deep sigh and a pronounced smile. "I never knew communing with nature could be so peaceful."

"Peacetime is over," she said, and she leaned on the push pole and sent the boat gliding up to a dock. "Welcome to Blackhawk Landing."

Charly tied the boat.

"Forgive me," Avery said, "but we used two different types of transportation just to have lunch on a broken-down pier?"

"Oh, ye of little faith," she teased, and took his hand. "The bayou is full of secrets."

Charly stopped once to allow a king snake to pass. "Blackhawk was a Cherokee Indian who loved an Acadian from Nova Scotia."

"That's not much of a story," he said as they wove through some overgrown vines.

"Do you want the facts, or the fiction-based-on-fact story?"

"Fiction, definitely."

When they emerged from the woods, Charly presented the tattered structure before them as if it were one of the finest castles in Europe.

"I take it Bob Vila hasn't been by yet."

She gave him a playful swat. "Originally, there was a second floor with a wraparound porch. It was designed with twenty-four windows on either side to catch the cross breezes." She took him in through the front hallway, then to what had once been the parlor. Several milk crates sat next to the crumbled remains of the fireplace.

"Is this place safe?"

"Sure. We've been coming here for years," she said. Charly upended three of the crates and blew off the dust and cobwebs. Then she arranged them like a small table for two before reaching for the picnic basket.

"You didn't pack that," he said when she had spread a napkin over the center crate. "I'll bet you can't even make a sandwich."

"You'd win that one. Odelle did all the work."

"And you took the credit."

He came close, reaching around her to inventory the sandwiches and other goodies. Charly's fingers struggled with the plastic wrap as his thighs brushed hers. The temperature seemed to be rising and the air grew thick.

"Is there a problem?" he practically purred against her ear.

"Yes. No. I mean—"

He silenced her by lifting her hair away from her neck and blowing his warm breath against her skin. Her eyes closed and she bit the inside of her cheek to keep from moaning out loud. No response was her best weapon.

"What are you thinking right now?" he asked as his lips tasted her skin. His hand slipped around her, his fingers splayed against her abdomen.

"I'm wondering if these extra sandwiches Odelle made for your girlfriend will keep."

He pulled back as if he'd been burned. Served him right.

"Girlfriend?"

Charly busied herself by arranging drinks. "It seems Odelle has seen the same woman I saw the other night. Are you going to tell me it was all in my imagination again?"

"It isn't what you're thinking."

Charly met his dark gaze. "I wouldn't be thinking about it at all if you hadn't…"

He gave her a boyish grin. "Can I help it if I find you irresistible?"

"Nice try. Look, I know you went out of your way last night, and I appreciate it."

His grin turned wolfish.

She held up a hand. "I don't show my appreciation that way. Here in the bayou, if you poach in someone else's territory, you can get shot."

"It isn't like that," he protested. "Really."

"Fine," she said, more to end the uncomfortable conversation than from real conviction. "Sit down and eat. I'll tell you all about Blackhawk and Noelle."

Avery took his seat, grabbed one of the sandwiches and looked over at her expectantly. "I'm all ears."

No, you're all raw masculinity and blatant sexuality. Charly nibbled a grape as she gathered her scattered thoughts. "Noelle was only fifteen when her family was forced out of Canada. They were traveling toward Louisiana with others who'd been similarly deposed, when they were attacked by a roaming band of Indians."

"I think I saw this on the late show."

Charly threw a grape at him. He caught it and popped it into his mouth. "Noelle was an incredible beauty. She had hair the color of night and eyes the color of a storm."

"Sounds like she could have been a Delacroix."

Flustered, Charly asked, "Are you going to keep interrupting me?"

"Sorry."

"In no time, the mighty warrior Blackhawk fell in love with Noelle."

"And they lived happily ever after?"

Charly gave him a stern look. "No. Noelle's father had formed a rescue party and attacked the Indians. The Indians were defenseless against the rifles. Noelle's father was just about to kill Blackhawk when Noelle threw herself in the path of the oncoming bullet."

"He killed his own daughter?"

"She didn't die immediately, but it didn't look good. Noelle's father was beside himself."

"Understandable."

"She opened her eyes and found the two men she loved at her bedside. She said she would only fight for her life if the two of them would agree to share her."

"And *then* they lived happily ever after?"

"Noelle died. Her father announced that he was taking her body with him for burial. Blackhawk followed because he wanted to be close to her spirit. He built this house and spent the next fifty years waiting to join her."

Avery sighed. "That's pretty depressing."

Charly smiled. "True love often is."

One brow arched questioningly. "So you're cynical about love, too?"

She shrugged. "Let's just say that I've seen the destructive power of love firsthand."

"Marie and Jax seem happily married."

She nodded. "Beau, Shelby and I are the last. Though if Travis has his way, Shelby'll be off to Texas in no time."

"So your aversion to love doesn't have anything to do with your siblings?"

"I would hardly call it an aversion."

"I'm guessing it has something to do with your parents."

She froze. "Leave it alone."

He whistled. "At least I understand now why you're so tough on your father and you hardly mention your mother."

"I'm not going to discuss my parents," Charly said

between clenched teeth. "I'm not some emotional cripple, so just drop it."

He got down on the floor and leaned his back against the crate, crossing his long legs at the ankles. "I was lucky."

"Why?"

"My folks make Ozzie and Harriet look like they had a bad marriage."

Charly smiled, and some of her anger drained away. "White picket fence and the whole nine yards?"

"Right down to the lawn ornaments," he quipped.

"Then how come you left your hometown? Why didn't you just settle down with the girl next door?"

He shrugged. "I needed to breathe."

Charly shook her head. "How did we get so maudlin? This was supposed to be a fun picnic."

"It is," he said, and reached out his hand to her. "Come here."

She was balancing on the tightrope between "should" and "want." *Want* was more powerful. *Should* was right. "I've already explained how I feel about that."

"Please?" he said softly, both arms outstretched.

CHAPTER NINE

"I SHOULDN'T."

Her voice was little more than a whisper. Marshall agreed in theory, only his body wasn't much concerned with theory at the moment.

"Just for a minute or two," he urged.

The look in her eyes intrigued him. Budding passion was evident, but he saw something else. Something disturbing. "You look like the proverbial doe caught in the headlights," he said.

"Maybe because my brain wants one thing and my body has a different idea."

He couldn't help but smile as he rose to his feet. Did she realize what her admission did to him? "You're great for a guy's ego."

"As if yours needs any help." She flushed but didn't retreat when he took her hand and pulled her up from the crate. "We should think about this, Avery."

He reached out and brushed a wayward strand of ebony hair from her cheek. "I'm glad you mentioned thinking." His fingers moved to her throat, to the spot where her pulse beat erratically. "I don't seem to think clearly when you're around." He pushed the curve of hair behind her ear and nuzzled her neck. Her palms flattened against his chest. "My plan is to kiss you."

"You have a plan?" The pitch of her voice was unnaturally high.

"Mmm-hmm," he murmured. "I'm hoping that once I put it into action, I can stop thinking about it."

He bent lower to kiss the sensitive spot beneath her earlobe. He heard her deep breath, felt her muscles constrict. With his hand on her softly rounded hips, he opened his legs and cradled her small body against his. His own reaction was immediate and obvious. He felt her stiffen in his arms.

He lifted his head and searched her face. Conflict clouded her beautiful eyes. *Slow down,* he urged himself as he took her hand and brought it to his mouth. His eyes locked with hers and he kissed the vulnerable underside of her wrist. Her response was an honest, spontaneous little cry. Guilt was no match for his desire, so he dismissed his conscience and slipped his hand around her waist.

Her uncertainty fueled his need. He pulled her shirt from the waistband of her jeans and smiled when he felt the tremor rush through her.

"Avery?"

"Hush," he urged. "I'm not planning on doing anything more than some heavy necking. Okay?"

He held his breath until she gave the smallest nod of consent. She smiled then, lifting her arms to circle his neck. Her innocent action caused her breasts to flatten against his chest. Need, stronger than he had ever experienced, electrified him.

He bent his head and kissed her with deliberate tenderness. It was like sinking slowly into warm quicksand. He was no longer sure that his legs would support him. He didn't stop to think, he just reacted.

He maneuvered her to the ground until they were both kneeling. Then he held her tightly as he lay back, pulling her on top of him. He could feel every curve, every inch of her body. A body he'd fantasized about night after night.

Charly lifted her head and grinned. "Did you buy a bigger knife?"

He laughed. "Obviously I'm happy to see you."

His fingers entwined in her hair and he guided her mouth to his. When he parted his lips and invited her inside, she didn't hesitate. She was temptation and redemption. There was something about the way she responded to him that made him feel so very male.

Charly broke the seal of their lips and reached for the buttons of his shirt, but he didn't miss the slight tremble in her hand.

"Charly?"

"I just want to look," she whispered. She seemed completely fascinated as her dainty fingertips brushed his shirt aside. When she moved to straddle him, Marshall nearly groaned from the sheer, unexpected pleasure.

Her hands were everywhere at once. Each place she touched, she kissed. He was dying, but was it ever sweet!

When he could no longer stand it, he slid his hand beneath her shirt, reached up and cupped her breast. Her lips parted on a rush of breath and her head fell back. He yanked the rest of her shirt free, then pushed it up, both hands molding her exquisite body. He touched her nipples through the lacy fabric of her bra. His thumbs caressed slowly, deliberately, until he coaxed a response.

She moved rhythmically with his touch. The feel of her small body so close, yet completely unattainable, was a heady sensation. He heard a drumming in his ears as he bent forward and kissed the taut peak straining against the fabric. She made the most incredible sound, then went completely still.

"Charly?" He tried to make sense of what was happening. It was difficult for reason to penetrate his passion-fogged brain.

"Button your shirt!" she yelled, scrambling to her feet and stuffing her shirt haphazardly into her jeans. "Hurry!"

"What is it?" he asked as he got to his feet. Movement was pretty uncomfortable. His body was a little slow getting the message that they were finished.

Charly was frantically trying to smooth her shirt and her hair in one confused motion. Her cheeks were flushed and he definitely thought she had that just-kissed look.

An instant later, so did her brother.

"You're a dead man," Beau said as he yanked off his tie.

"Beau!" Charly screamed. "Don't you dare!"

Beau seemed undeterred. "When I finish with you, Avery, they won't even be able to identify you with dental records." He took another long stride forward, his fists balled and ready.

Marshall braced for the attack, silently acknowledging that he deserved it—and then some.

"Get out of here, Charly."

With the same boldness he'd witnessed when she'd waded into the swamp, she rushed forward and plowed, arms straight in front of her, into her much larger brother. Apparently Beau had been unprepared for the move. She managed to knock him off balance, a situation he quickly rectified.

When he grabbed her arm and gave a yank, Charly cried out in pain. Marshall moved with the speed of light.

"Boys!" she called, sandwiched between them. "You're hurting me!"

Marshall stumbled back, taking her along with him. Her feet dangled in the air as he held her against him.

"Stay right there," she warned her brother.

"I'm sorry I twisted your bad arm," Beau said. "Now get the hell out of here. Avery and I have business."

Beau's eyes were angry gray slits. Marshall was torn between a strong desire to punch the guy into the next parish for hurting Charly and letting Beau pummel him for fooling with his kid sister. *Lord, what a mess!*

"I'm not asking you, Beau. I'm insisting. Now, you will leave immediately. Go!"

"Just as soon as I rearrange his face."

Beau stepped forward and Charly held her arms out. "You'll have to hurt me to get to him. You don't want to do that *again,* do you?"

Beau winced as if she had slapped him. "I'm sorry Charly, it was an accident."

"I'm not going to let you hurt him," she warned.

Marshall gently lowered Charly to the ground, "Can I say something?"

"No!" they screamed in unison.

He turned Charly around and lifted her chin. "I think you should do what your brother says."

"But—"

He placed his finger against her lips. "It's okay. Really." He smiled and gave her a wink.

"But Beau will—" she sputtered.

"Beau and I will come to an understanding."

"You'll understand what it feels like to pick your teeth off the floor," Beau grumbled.

"I'll only leave if you promise me you won't hurt him," she said to her brother.

"He won't hurt me," Marshall assured her. "Now go. I'll meet you back where we left the horses."

"Beau Delacroix," she began, walking up to her brother and wagging her finger in his face. "If you hurt him, I swear I will kill you in your sleep."

"Get going, Charly."

She let out an exasperated sigh and looked at Marshall imploringly, but he only shrugged. Throwing her hands into the air, she shouted, "I give up! If you two want to beat each other senseless, feel free."

"Well?" Marshall asked conversationally.

Beau's lips twitched in a menacing smile. "I'm gonna enjoy this."

CHARLY WENT TO HER BEDROOM, closed the door and fell onto the bed. She bent one arm over her closed eyes. Anger, guilt and a decent amount of physical frustration took turns churning her stomach. Fragmented thoughts bounced around inside her head. She concentrated on taking deep, relaxing breaths.

After several minutes, her consciousness floated between sleep and reality. Images wafted in and out. Avery's seductive smile taunted her. Beau's angry words assailed her. Then she saw the eyes.

Her head snapped up. Her heart was racing, pounding against her ribs. Unexplainable fear brought a tightness to her chest, making each breath an effort. ''The eyes,'' she whispered to the empty room.

She sat up and rubbed her face, trying to concentrate. In one flicker of memory, the eyes were far away. In another, they were close. But there was no face. Charly experienced that annoying awareness that something important was just beyond her grasp. "Eyes," she repeated like a mantra. "Eyes." Nothing.

"I'm losing it," she grumbled, deciding what she really needed was to splash cold water on her face.

The memory hit her so hard that she stumbled back against the bed. She was outside Swampy's bar. A breeze carried the stale smell of beer. Frank was smiling as he got out of the cruiser. Then the image twirled in her mind, spinning and changing form like the colors in a kaleidoscope. Frank's smile transformed into an expression of shock, then terror in the seconds after the shot. Charly cried out in absolute anguish as her mind replayed his face at the instant the bullet pierced his body. The image came time and again.

"Charly?" Avery said, bursting through the door.

He was followed by Beau. They both looked at her with concern.

She blinked, working her way out of the quagmire

of her memories. Avery came over and knelt by her bedside. He took her hands in his and searched her face. "You screamed. What happened?"

She shook her head. "Nothing, really."

Beau came to sit next to her, wrapping one arm around her shoulder. "Jeez, kid, you're shaking like a leaf. What happened?"

Charly managed a smile. "I'm fine, really." She pushed Avery away with a little more force than intended and stood to escape Beau's smothering protection. Glancing down, she realized that her hands *were* shaking. Defensively, she shoved them into the pockets of her jeans.

Careful to keep her eyes fixed on a neutral point off in space, she said, "I see you two managed to come to some kind of agreement without behaving like barroom brawlers."

Avery stood up beside her. "Forget about us. What's going on with you?"

"I must have nodded off," she told him. "I can't believe I let a dream spook me. I must be really tired or something."

"Or something," Avery repeated skeptically.

"Charly, Jada was looking for you," Beau said. "She was pretty upset. That's why I made the trip out to Blackhawk looking for you."

"Why didn't you say so before?" Charly cried. She went to the bedside table and stabbed at the keypad to enter Jada's number. The machine picked up on the fourth ring. "It's Charly. Call me." She glanced at the clock, then dialed the bank where Jada worked.

"Miss Crowley's office."

"This is Charly Delacroix. Is she in?"

"Why, um, no," the secretary stammered. "We've been trying to reach her for hours."

"What do you mean, *hours?*" she demanded, gripping the receiver with both hands.

"I assumed she was going out to see you. Her daddy is frantic. She isn't answering her cell phone and she hasn't responded to her pager."

"What makes you think she was coming out here?" Charly asked.

"Well—" the secretary paused "—because she said, 'She needs me,' just before she went tearing out of here."

CHAPTER TEN

"CAN'T YOU DRIVE any faster?" Charly snapped. "I knew you would just slow me down."

"Someone has to," Avery grumbled.

She glared at his profile. "You sound like Beau. I can't tell you how happy I am that the two of you 'bonded' without a fistfight. Though it would have served you right for trying to seduce me."

"Hey?" His hand closed over her thigh. "I know you're worried about your friend, but don't start slinging nasty accusations my way. I don't deserve them."

Charly winced. "I'm sorry."

"Apology accepted."

Shoving the hair out of her eyes, she leaned back in the bucket seat. Her face was illuminated by the lights on the dashboard and the wind rippled the fabric of her shirt.

"Which way?" he asked as they came to the intersection.

"Right, then right again at the first traffic light."

Charly drummed her fingers against the trim along the windshield. She vacillated between the embarrassing conviction that they would find Jada relaxing at home with a martini in one hand, the latest issue of

Cosmo in the other, and sheer terror that something horrible had happened to her.

"That's it!" she said excitedly. "The big one up on the hill."

She scarcely gave Marshall a chance to set the emergency brake before she leapt from the car and raced for the door. Nerves caused her to fumble with her key ring. Her heart was pounding in her ears when she finally calmed down enough to slip the key into the lock.

"Avery!" she yelped when she saw him come up beside her with a gun.

"Stay behind me." The words came out as a steely command.

"I have to disable the alarm," she argued, trying to push past his big body. It would have been easier to try to change the flow of the Mississippi.

His arm arched, pressing her against the open door. "What alarm?" he whispered.

She listened for a minute. No short warning beeps. Her heart fell to her feet. The alarm system had been turned off. "We have to go in."

"I'll go in," he said. "You go back to the car and call the authorities."

She wanted to argue, but common sense told her not to bother. Besides, Avery was right. If something had happened to Jada, the sooner they got it out over the wires, the better.

Positioning herself so that she could watch the front and side of the huge brick home, she grabbed her car phone and called the station house directly.

"This is Charly Delacroix. Patch me through to Jake."

"He's off duty," the dispatcher said.

"It's an emergency. Is he at home?"

"Yes, ma'am. Do you need help?"

She gave the address to the dispatcher, then cleared the line and called Jake at home.

"Hello?"

"Hi, Annabelle, this is Charly," she explained quickly. "Is Jake there?"

"Yes, he is," her cousin said. "I'll get him for you."

Charly gave an abbreviated version of the problem to Bayou Beltane's chief of police. "So I don't know whether Jada's in real trouble or not, but I can't risk it. It's not like her just to disappear like this. Can you get over here right away?"

"I'm on my way," Jake promised. "Meanwhile, you stay on the line with Annabelle until one of the units arrives."

Charly swallowed her groan. "That isn't necessary," she said. "I've got to see about Avery. Bye."

Ignoring Jake's protest, Charly severed the connection and scurried to the trunk of her car. Alert to her surroundings, she took a few seconds longer than usual to load her pistol. Adrenaline coursed through her system. She didn't know why she felt this rush of fear, but she felt sure it had something to do with Jada's past history with Mason Ranier.

The click seemed deafeningly loud when she gripped the butt of the gun between her palms. Training took over as she tried to push thoughts of her dear friend's face to the back of her mind. Nothing could happen to Jada. Please!

Her body hugged the bushes as she checked the exterior of the house. Nocturnal insects chirped and screeched at irregular intervals, as if they could sense the anxiety coiled in her gut. Stepping over a garden hose, she took a breath, held it, then stepped out into the open. Her gun was on him in a second. Her finger flinched against the trigger.

"Damn it, Charly! I could have blown your head off!"

"I thought you were inside the house!" She lowered her weapon but kept the two-handed grip for readiness. "Any sign of her?"

"Nope."

The stillness of the night was rent by the sudden blast of sirens. The stench of burned rubber filled the air as no fewer than three patrol cars came to a screeching halt in and around the driveway.

"Drop 'em!"

Like mirror images, Charly and Avery raised their hands with their respective weapons dangling from a single finger.

"It's okay," Jake said, striding purposefully toward them. "Find anything?" he asked as he bent down and brushed Charly's cheek with a kiss.

"Nothing so far. We've checked the exterior of the house. The alarm system's been deactivated."

Jake's brow furrowed into deep lines. His eyes moved to Avery. "You're the personal trainer?"

Avery glanced at Charly questioningly.

"Marshall Avery, Jake Trahan," she said. "Jake's married to my cousin Annabelle."

"I should have guessed you were a relative," Avery said, shoving his gun in the back of his jeans and offering his hand. "I'm starting to think there are a few too many branches in the Delacroix family tree."

Jake laughed. "All right, Charly. We'll go in and check out your friend's house."

It took less than thirty minutes for Jake and his men to determine that there was nothing suspicious in the house. No evidence of a struggle, no blood, nothing out of the ordinary.

"I'll be happy to put a want out on her car," Jake said.

Charly gave him a hug, and he hurried out the door. "I'm going to call home and see if there's been any message from Jada," she said.

She went to the kitchen and grabbed the telephone off the wall. Absently, she toyed with one of the pens stacked in a ceramic vase that matched the muted peach that she had often joked was Jada's signature color. There had been no word. Not at Riverwood. Not at Buster Crowley's house.

"Was that her father you were talking to?" Avery asked as he joined her.

"He's concerned. He said that Jada has been acting funny ever since the wedding."

Avery shrugged, then hoisted himself up onto the counter. "It stands to reason that she could get spooked by a bomb going off." He looked around, nodding as he took in the decorator touches and the Sub-Zero refrigerator. "Nice digs. But then—" he paused, flashing that killer smile "—this *is* Barbie's dream house."

"I'm going to check her answering machine," she told him.

Avery followed her up the wrought-iron stairway, which appeared to be floating in the center of the living room. He made a few appreciative sounds as they walked to the master bedroom. The machine was on the edge of a professional makeup table that dominated the dressing area.

"Sunless tanning lotion, age-defying cream, night therapy." Avery read off the labels as he picked up a few of the items on the table. "It sure takes a lot of chemicals to be a natural beauty."

Charly gave him a stern look. "Stop mauling her stuff." Then she felt her brows draw together as she looked at the answering machine. "That's weird."

"What?"

"There aren't any messages."

"So?"

She looked up and met his dark gaze. "There should be, I left one myself not an hour ago."

She could almost see his mind working. "I guess you're sure that you had the right number?"

"I know Jada's voice."

He lifted the machine, then popped open the compartment where the tape stored calls. "Remote."

"Excuse me?"

"This model allows you to call in from an outside line, enter a code and collect your messages."

"How do you get the code?"

"You assign it yourself. Is there anyone Jada would have given it to?"

"No. I don't think so."

"Then we have to assume that Jada cleared the machine."

Charly found that idea comforting. Abruptly, she got up and went into the bathroom. "You might just be on to something," she called.

"What did you find?"

She studied the contents of the medicine cabinet. Fear was quickly being replaced by curiosity. "It's what I *can't* find."

He crowded into the small space with her. His chest brushed against her back, his breath rustled her hair. By sheer force of will, Charly was able to speak in a normal tone. "Jada's makeup and curlers are gone."

"What's all that stuff out on the table?"

The mere sound of his voice was enough to jack her temperature up a few degrees. He didn't even have to touch her for her body to react to him. It wasn't fair!

"That's nothing," Charly said, ducking away from him before she gave in to the strong urge to rip his shirt off. "Women are conditioned from birth to buy cosmetics. Every female I know has a drawer or a shelf devoted to products that don't work or aren't the right color. The hoarding of unwanted cosmetics will continue until we learn to throw them away or until they get better lighting in stores."

Avery laughed. "Five bucks says you don't have a shelf or a drawer."

Charly felt her cheeks burn. "You're right, of course," she admitted, eyes averted. "I figure why waste good money on something that won't do any good?''

She almost made a clean getaway. Almost. He took her by the shoulders and forced her to meet his gaze. She kept her spine stiff, telling herself that she didn't want a repeat of the explosive passion they had shared at the landing.

But the feel of his thumbs grazing her cheekbones and the warm wash of minty breath against her face was nearly impossible to resist. An overpowering need seemed to start in her gut and spread, until she felt it in every cell of her body. Desire came in such a fierce rush that she actually felt dizzy.

He rested his forehead against hers. "You have to learn to look at yourself more objectively. Not to mention positively."

She blinked. Here she was, ready and willing for mad, passionate sex, and the man decides to give her a pep talk on self-esteem. The irony made her laugh. Her own idiocy made her want to cry. So the man had kissed her a few times. So what? When had she forgotten that Avery was out of her league?

"You're right," she said with forced lightness. "I should stop making remarks about my lack of feminine attributes."

The frown reached his eyes. "Feminine isn't bows and lace, Charly. Anyone who can't see you're a woman isn't looking in the right places."

"I don't—"

"Delacroix?"

At the sound of her name, she and Avery jumped

apart like two teenagers caught in the act. "Chief Harrington?" she stammered.

Hoisting his utility belt, the chief replaced his revolver, then adjusted the belt on his hips. Charly knew it was merely a delaying tactic he used when he wanted to size up a situation. And judging from the disgusted look on his face, he didn't think much of finding her in Jada's bedroom, embracing her personal trainer.

"I heard the call on my radio. They mentioned you had phoned it in."

"What are you doing here?" Avery asked. "The door was…"

Charly broke in quickly. "What he means, Chief, is that there's no real problem that we know of yet, and I called Jake because he's my cousin's husband."

Harrington scowled at the implication, and Charly heard the distinct sound of her career aspirations crashing and burning. "Please excuse him. I appreciate your concern, Chief."

Avery rubbed his side as the two men exchanged resentful stares. Sighing loudly, Charly decided it was in her best interest to end this standoff as soon as possible. "I'm sorry you came so far out of your way," she said to her boss, then took Avery's elbow and used it like a rudder to direct him out of the room.

"For nothing," Harrington grumbled. "Your call pulled three units off patrol. I would have thought you'd jump at an opportunity like this, Officer."

Inwardly, Charly groaned. Outwardly, she kept her wooden smile in place. "Opportunity?" she asked.

Harrington preceded them down the hallway. The jingle of metal handcuffs marked each step. "You should have taken the initiative, Delacroix. Investigated before you called men off the job. You still have arrest powers, even if you're on sick leave.''

She glared at Avery as she followed her boss to the front door. The two men exited while she went to the keypad and reset the alarm.

''Where did he go?'' she wailed when she found Avery alone in the yard.

''Chief Personality bolted.''

Her shoulders slumped. ''Wonderful. Just wonderful.''

SHE COULD NO LONGER HEAR him in the next room. Well, she hadn't exactly heard *him*. It was more like the occasional squeak of a mattress coil or a faint thud.

Charly paced her room, raw with emotion. Harrington was such a pig! If she had ''taken the initiative'' he probably would have given her hell for acting without proper police authority. Lord, but the man found fault with her every action.

She had tried to sleep for what felt like hours, but the moment her eyes had closed, the nightmare came.

Shaking it off, desperate to think about something else, she moved over to the window, and that's when she saw them—Avery and his mystery woman huddled together by the pool.

It made her blood boil to think he was that low, that despicable. Carrying on with her while he... ''I should have let Beau knock his teeth out. I wonder if Miss Pool Babe will come running at all hours of the day and night when he has to gum his food?''

She was very close to blind rage when she made her

decision. If she couldn't sleep, she might as well share some of her bad karma.

Pulling on her robe, she quietly walked out into the hall to Avery's room. Her fingers closed around the knob, twisting it by half degrees, fully expecting to find the door locked.

It wasn't.

Charly didn't even have the chance to scream. His hand clamped down over her mouth and she was carried inside the room. She felt the cold steel of his gun pressed against her cheek.

He dumped her on the bed and stood above her, scratching his chin. His shirt was open. His feet were bare. But it was his jeans that drew her eyes. The top button was open. The thick mat of dark hair that covered his chest tapered to a thin line before slipping beneath the waist of his jeans. It might as well have been a big neon arrow. Charly swallowed, hard.

He went to the nightstand and placed his gun in the top drawer. When he returned, he stood with his feet braced apart, his expression hard. "It's two in the morning."

"I know what time it is," she hissed, sitting up and straightening her robe. "Why did you do that to me?"

"To you? What are you doing sneaking into my room?"

She bristled. "I wasn't sneaking. I wanted to talk to you."

His hair was mussed, as if he had been running his fingers through the dark mass. "That would be a change from dinner. You wouldn't even look at me, let alone utter a civil word."

"I was mad."

His mouth became a tight line. "Maybe your father is willing to overlook your spoiled, nasty outbursts, but I'm not. At twenty-five, you ought to be able to communicate your feelings in an adult fashion."

"Fine." She stood up, annoyed that she had to tilt her head back to maintain eye contact. "I'd like to *communicate* that I don't appreciate you pawing me, then calling your girlfriend for a quickie by the pool."

His eyes narrowed and his expression was as cold as stone. "I've already explained that."

She balled her hands into fists at her side. "You haven't explained squat, Avery. Not the woman, the clothes, the watch—" she turned and eyed the closed drawer "—or the gun."

He let out a breath. "Okay. She's a business associate. Since I'm here on a job, I asked her to come here at night so it wouldn't interfere with my time with you."

She felt her anger being replaced by frustration. "Still pretty evasive. And being evasive is the same as lying."

He threw his arms up. "*I'm* evasive, huh? Take a look in the mirror, darlin'."

They stood toe to toe. "I'll have you know that most people think I'm *too* blunt."

"Most people don't know you!"

"And you do?"

"I'll tell you what I know," he said in an urgent whisper. "I know that something about your parents' divorce has screwed you up."

She opened her mouth, then closed it.

"I know that you take potshots at your father because you're too scared to let him know what you're really angry about."

"I'm scared?"

"Yes." The syllable spilled from his tightly clenched teeth. "You're scared of a lot of things. I can see right through you, Charly." His whole demeanor changed with the last statement. The fury seemed to drain away, replaced by a gut-wrenching kindness that tugged at her heart. "You're afraid to be a woman." He took her face in his hands and lowered his head toward hers. "You're afraid of this."

The kiss was sweet and brutally tender. He seemed to sense just what she needed. And after listening to the painful truth about herself, she needed him. Needed to feel the way he was cherishing her with his lips. She clung to him, drawing on his strength.

Being in his arms, being with him felt so right. Her mind struggled for an explanation, some logical reason why he made her feel so alive, so whole.

He ended the kiss slowly, then set her back from him. When he flashed that smile, she found it contagious. She waited for her pulse to return to normal before attempting to speak. "You're pretty astute, Avery."

"Told you I was a bright guy."

Absently, she touched her mouth as she strode to the window and looked out without seeing. "Am I really terrible to Daddy?" She wished Avery was still holding her. That she could still smell his scent, feel his strength.

"Only when you jab him about your childhood."

"I'll bet Ozzie and Harriet Avery didn't put their needs above yours."

"No," he answered softly. "But I was their only shot at perfection."

Charly nodded. "I guess there is safety in numbers. Beau caught hell for not following in the family tradition. Doing an MBA instead of a juris doctorate was—in Daddy's opinion—a form of heresy. When Marie dropped out of medical school to study aromatherapy, I thought Daddy would have a stroke. By the time I decided to bag law school, he was okay. Until I went to the police academy."

"Put yourself in his place," Avery reasoned. "He just doesn't want anything to happen to you."

"His concern is touching. Ten years late, but touching."

"That's what I'm talking about," he said, gently taking her shoulders and turning her to him. "What did he do ten years ago that was so terrible that you're still punishing him?"

"You wouldn't understand."

"Try me," he coaxed.

"He let her leave."

"Your mother?"

She nodded. "He didn't even put up a fight. He was too busy working. She took me all the way to Colorado. I could hear her crying at night. She kept a picture of him in her dresser. I used to stand in the hallway and watch her. She would hug that picture with tears streaming down her face."

"Sometimes people just stop loving each other, Charly."

She laughed without humor. "That's the piece you're missing."

"I don't follow."

"It would have been okay if they hated each other. I probably could have dealt with that. Daddy wouldn't come visit me because it was too painful for him to be in the same state as my mother. Mother devoted herself to her art gallery, working until she dropped so that she wouldn't have the energy to think about him. My parents' love for each other destroyed both of them."

"Maybe you should try to see their relationship through adult eyes."

Charly's shoulders slumped. Suddenly she felt terribly tired. She didn't want to fight or think or remember anymore, so she reached for him instead. "Maybe I'd like to communicate another way now."

"We can't," he said. "Or rather we can, but we shouldn't."

Boldly, she stepped forward and rubbed her body against his.

He seemed to waver, uttering an expletive before saying, "Okay, Charly. You win."

She looked into his eyes. "I didn't realize we were having a competition."

Avery's face was a study in raw emotion. "I thought I could be satisfied with simple kisses. I bet myself that I was strong enough to control this." He gazed down at her with smoldering eyes. "I'm not."

Reaching up, she cupped his cheek in her palm. "There's something I think you should know."

He placed his finger against her lips and drew her tighter into the cradle of his thighs. Any doubts she might have had regarding his desire were instantly dispelled. He greedily pushed aside the collar of her robe and kissed her throat until Charly actually shivered. He was moving fast, inspiring an onslaught of turbulent sensation that had her spinning. "Really, Avery," she pleaded with an unsteady breath. "I have to tell you—"

"Hush," he murmured, his hand coming up to test the weight of her breast through the fabric. "Now is the time for actions, not words."

"But—"

He pulled her hard against him. "I've been dying to touch you again," he whispered.

Her mind reeled as his hands swept through her hair, down her back to her hips. Lowering his mouth, he kissed her deeply as he carried her to his bed.

She should have settled things first. She knew it was the right thing to do. But suddenly right and wrong didn't matter. The only thing that mattered was this almost painful desire to feel his warm body next to hers. The sheer intensity of her longing kicked in and Charly felt frantic. She fumbled desperately with his shirt.

"Slow down, darlin'." He laughed and took her wrists, tugging gently, then twisted her so that she was beneath him on the mattress. "We've got all night."

Desire surged through her, filling her with fierce impatience. "Take your shirt off."

He chuckled at the demand behind her breathy request. "Ladies first." In one easy motion he parted her robe. A low rumble sounded in his throat when he dipped his head to take her nipple into his mouth.

Her hands fell away from his shirt. She grabbed fist-fuls of the bedspread as wave after wave of new sensation exploded through her. When his teeth grazed her skin, Charly thought she might die then and there. She wanted something, everything. "Avery, I..."

His head came up and his ebony eyes locked on hers. "Use my name."

Charly threw her head back, frustration coiling in her stomach. "I don't like your name."

Her skin was damp and small shudders claimed her as his big hands stroked her feverish body. "Say my name, Charly."

Her only response was an animallike moan. She was writhing beneath him. Frantically, her small hands touched and tugged. He had her completely naked in a matter of seconds. He smelled her shampoo, tasted the salty slickness of her skin. Her eyes, all smoky and heavy-lidded with passion, urged him on. She moved and responded to his every caress as if she had never before been touched. No woman had ever made him feel so much a man.

He left her only long enough to shed his clothes. Charly was with him. She reared up, wrapping that beautiful naked body against him. Her breasts pressed against his back as she kissed his neck and shoulders.

He flipped her over into his lap. She was temptation personified, and seeing her need, he kissed her with a controlled savagery that surprised even him.

"I need to be inside of you."

"Yes."

He lifted her, then pushed her down on the mattress once again. "Say it."

Her hands grasped his hips and she arched toward him. "Hurry."

Using his body, he pried her thighs apart. He held her gaze. "Say my name."

"Please...Marshall!"

He drove inside her in one motion. Then stopped. Shock and disbelief assailed him when she cried out. "Damn it, Charly, hold still!"

"Why?"

Gritting his teeth, Marshall felt beads of perspiration form on his brow as he struggled for some measure of self-control. Charly thwarted his intentions when she began to move rhythmically beneath him. "Stop it! I'll hurt you."

"No you won't," she murmured, her fingers biting into the flesh of his hips.

"Don't—"

Her tongue came out to flick his nipple, and Marshall gave in to his need. He took her, urgently plunging deep inside her, building quickly to match her frenzied passion.

He filled her, stretched her, loved her. Her hands stroked the sweat-slicked muscles of his back. Her fingers fluttered over the valley of his spine. Her palms cupped him, urged him deeper.

She strained against him, clinging to him, wrapping her legs around his waist. He felt her climax, then his consciousness dimmed as he exploded inside her.

Drained, Marshall collapsed to the side as wave after wave of remorse washed over him. "I'm sorry, Charly."

"Sorry?" she repeated in a voice almost too faint to hear.

"You should have told me."

She rolled against him, draping one shapely leg across his thigh. Her fingertip traced the outline of his rib cage. "It's no big deal, Avery."

Resting one arm over his head, he cursed himself. "I must have hurt you. I wouldn't have been so—"

"If I'm not complaining, why are you?"

How was he supposed to answer that? Shifting his weight, he turned so that he could see her face. He brushed a few strands of hair off her cheek. Her skin was flushed and her smile was purely sinful. "I wasn't complaining. I just wasn't prepared for this little surprise."

Her smile faded. "I wasn't...satisfying? I thought that because I felt so...free, that—" Charly moved away from him.

He grabbed her arm before she could flee. "I wasn't giving a critique," he said, tipping her chin up until he could see her sultry eyes. "I just don't understand how this happened."

"I came to your room and basically threw myself at you."

He heard the sting in her voice. Gently, he pulled her into the circle of his arms. "I was just on my way to your room when you showed up."

"Really?" Her hand fluttered across his chest.

"Charly, I'm only human. And now that I know how human you are, I don't get it. Why haven't you been with a man before?"

It was hard for him to remain calm when she started raking her nails through his chest hair.

"I haven't been able to trust anyone before. Thank you, Avery. You made it perfect."

He closed his eyes. God, what a mess. Now he had no choice but to tell her the truth.

CHAPTER ELEVEN

"YOU HAVE TO STOP THAT," he insisted, grabbing her hands.

Startled by his harsh tone, she inched away from him. A sudden attack of modesty had her reaching for the sheet, followed by anxiety when she noted the grim expression on his face.

"Don't get strange, Avery. I've already told you it isn't a big deal. It had to happen sometime."

He got up and pulled on his jeans, then passed her her robe. "I have a feeling you're going to want to be dressed when you hear what I have to say."

When she had the belt secured in a knot, she moved up behind him. He was sitting on the edge of the bed, his head resting in his open hands. She wrapped her arms around his broad shoulders and kissed his ear playfully. "Lighten up, Avery. I'm not going to let you spoil this. Stop acting like you've committed a crime."

"I'm not a personal trainer."

Charly barely paused as she nibbled his earlobe. "So you're a gigolo. It's no wonder with the way you... jiggle."

He stood with enough force to push her back on her heels. Jamming his fists in his pockets, he turned and looked at her with blank eyes.

Alarms started ringing in her head. She sobered immediately. Moving to the edge of the bed, she sat properly and clasped her trembling hands in her lap. "What's worse than a gigolo?"

"Just let me say this, okay?"

"She's not your girlfriend," Charly gasped. "You're married?"

"Charly!"

"Right," she said. "I'll be quiet."

Minutes dragged like days as he paced, stroked his chin, then paced some more. Charly was ready to scream by the time he finally dropped to his knees before her and took her hands.

"I want you to know that this has nothing to do with what I'm about to tell you."

"This?"

"I made love to you because I wanted to."

Her mind flashed any number of possibilities. She swallowed the lump of fear clogging her throat.

"I'm not a personal trainer."

"You said that already," she snapped.

He flinched as if she'd struck him. "Sorry. I have been playing a role. But what I feel for you was never part of the deal."

Disaster was just around the corner. She saw it in his eyes, felt it in her chest. "I'm not going to like this, am I."

He closed his eyes and shook his head. "I'm in private security, Charly."

She let out the breath she'd been holding. "That's good," she said. "Between jobs you—"

"I'm not between jobs."

"You have to be," she insisted, ripping her hands from his and standing. Avery started toward her and she took several steps backward.

"I work for your father, Charly. He hired me to watch over you."

"Don't!" she shouted when he reached for her. "Don't...don't touch me." A rumble of cruel laughter bubbled up in her throat. "This is really funny. In a sick sort of way, of course." Her eyes bit into him. "All right Avery—if that *is* your real name—I don't care what lies you have to tell, and obviously you don't, either, but I want you out of here tomorrow."

"There's no reason for you to get—"

"Don't even start with that line, Avery. Did my father tell you which buttons to push? Is that how the two of you planned to 'handle' little Charly? Well, I'm tired of being handled. And worse than being handled, I can't stand being lied to. Tell my father that when you pick up your severance pay."

"Charly..."

"Back off," she warned, and somehow she managed to get out the door before the hot, angry tears fell. Numbly, she went to her room, opened the door and screamed.

"What?" Marshall demanded when he came up behind her.

Following her line of sight, he saw the shadowy figure slip out the window.

Justin came running. "Take care of her!" Marshall yelled as he pulled the gun from his jeans and disappeared out the window.

The figure was already sprinting around the edge of

the pool by the time Marshall lowered himself onto the drainpipe and dropped the twenty feet to the ground.

He came up, crouched and ready, gun pointed. Cursing, he ran in the direction where he had last seen the figure. Dew had turned the grass slick under his bare feet. Every one of his instincts was on full alert.

He reacted to every shadow, every flicker of movement. Then he heard the sound of a car engine. Dashing through the woods, he hurdled logs and slapped branches from his face even though he knew the probable outcome.

He burst out on the access road to the highway just in time to see the wink of red taillights speed out of sight.

He breathed deeply, filling his stinging lungs with the cool evening air before he let go with a string of curses. Then a twig cracked behind him. He raised his gun with rock-steady hands.

"It's just me!" Beau called as he stepped from the thick brush. "I was just heading back to my place when I saw the guy tearing across the back lawn. You didn't get him?"

"Does it look like I got him?"

"Next time," Beau said.

"There isn't going to be a next time," Marshall informed him. "I told Charly the truth."

"I think I mentioned that was not the way to go with her."

They headed back toward the house. "It was... necessary."

"Man-oh-man," Beau sighed. "I hope that doesn't mean what I think it means."

"Leave it alone."

"I would, if you'd left my baby sister alone."

Guilt, fierce and palpable, slumped his shoulders. "Your baby sister has made it clear that she doesn't want me here."

"I can change that."

Marshall stopped dead in his tracks. "Aren't you the guy who almost smashed in my face for kissing her?"

"Yep. But that was before I knew that she was in love with you."

Marshall snorted. "Forget love, she doesn't even like me after—"

"No details," Beau interrupted. "Knowing you did it is bad enough. If you tell me how, I'll have to kick your butt eight ways from Sunday." Beau grabbed him by the neck as if they were teammates planning strategy. "I'll only save you from the wrath of Charly if you give me your word that you aren't just amusing yourself."

"Not my style."

"Didn't think so." Beau whistled a tune the rest of the way up to the house.

Odelle greeted them at the kitchen door. Beau received a grandmotherly pat on the shoulder, Marshall a scorching glare. "Go tell your daddy to get Jake here," she said when they were inside. Bracing her hands on her hips, she added, "Two grown men running around in the woods half naked. I swear."

Marshall wasn't too thrilled to see the entire household seated around the kitchen table. His heart sank when it became painfully apparent that Charly wasn't even going to glance in his direction.

He and Beau took turns relating the story. Midway through their recital, Beau went to the refrigerator and tossed him a beer. He would have liked something stronger.

"The gall of that fool to think he can break in to Riverwood," Justin blustered. "Good thing you were around, Marshall. We owe you a lot."

"Actually," Charly began, "I know that—"

"I'm sorry, Dad," Beau cut in, "but when I found out that Marshall was here to protect Charly, I felt it was my duty to tell her who he really was."

Marshall watched Charly's angry face flame with color. "Beau," she said, "I can't believe—"

"Why, Charly, you know how impossible it is to keep a *secret* around here."

Beau's veiled meaning wasn't lost on his sister. Charly gave him a venomous look and her gaping mouth closed.

Justin took his youngest child's hands. "I'm sorry for the subterfuge, but I was sure you wouldn't cooperate if you knew the truth. I feel better knowing that Marshall is keeping an eye on you."

"Your little speech about hiring a personal trainer so that I could get back to work—was any of that the truth?"

"Try to see my side, Charly," Justin implored her. "I don't think I could stand it if you got hurt again. Seeing you in a coma, hooked up to all those tubes, was horrible for me."

"It wasn't exactly a walk in the park for me, either," she said. "Don't you have any faith in me? Is it so hard for you to believe that I'm actually good at what I do?''

''What you do is dangerous,'' Shelby observed. ''We worry about you. We love you.''

''Is that supposed to make lying to me okay?''

''No,'' her sister said with a pointed look at Justin. ''I'm glad Beau told you and I'm glad—''

''But—''

''But now we have to move on,'' Beau finished. ''I think Marshall should take Charly away. Someplace safe while the police try to find out who planted the bomb, and if the bomb is related to the calls, the break-in at her apartment and everything else that's been going on around here.''

Justin stood so quickly that his chair tumbled back, clattering against the floor. ''What calls? What happened to your apartment?''

Charly tossed Beau one of those thanks-for-nothing looks. ''He's blowing this all out of proportion. How exactly did you find out about the calls and the break-in?''

Beau shrugged. ''A friend.''

''Your brother is right,'' Justin thundered. ''You'll go someplace safe and—''

''I will not hide,'' Charly insisted.

''Let the authorities do their job,'' Shelby argued. ''You need to be somewhere out of harm's way.''

''Actually,'' Marshall said, holding Charly's cautious eyes, ''Charly's right. If we want to flush this guy out, our best shot is for her to stay where we can be pretty sure he'll come looking for her.''

She seemed momentarily confused by his defense. "Exactly."

"I absolutely forbid it!" Justin yelled.

"Hang on, Dad," Beau suggested. "It isn't as if she's vulnerable here. Marshall's proved he can look out for her."

Marshall hid his smile, impressed when he realized that this had been Beau's plan all along.

"True," Justin admitted after apparently giving the idea some thought. "I won't insist that you leave so long as you agree to follow Marshall's instructions."

"B-but—" Charly stammered.

"Your choice, kid," Beau said with soft challenge.

She stood, glaring daggers at the two of them. "What is that saying about the devil you know?"

She left them staring after her. When she had gone, Beau leaned close to Marshall and said, "On second thought, I don't think I did you much of a favor."

"HAS THERE BEEN ANY WORD?" Charly asked.

"I'm sorry, but Ms. Crowley still hasn't checked in."

"Thanks," she mumbled before replacing the receiver. Turning to Odelle, she shook her head sadly. "Jada hasn't called her father *or* her office. This isn't like her."

"Lot of that going around," Odelle opined, one brow arched accusingly. "Miss Jada isn't the only one round these parts acting a fool."

"She isn't acting," Beau said as he came through the door.

"You and I and sharp objects shouldn't be in the same room together," Charly warned.

He completely ignored her tone and bent to kiss her cheek. "Just looking out for your best interests."

"Odelle? Would you give Beau and me a minute alone, please?"

The housekeeper mumbled under her breath as she took a stack of laundry and headed for the second floor. Charly turned on him in every sense of the word. "Do you think Avery is the brother you never had? Do tell me why you sided with him last night and put me in an impossible position?"

Sighing, he went to the coffeemaker. "I think you put yourself in this position when you slept with the guy."

"Hush!" she screeched. "Did he run to you with pictures or what? You're the big brother, Beau. Your job description includes helping me get rid of the men I don't want around."

"Fair enough. Tell me why you don't want Marshall around."

She dragged him to the table, then pulled two chairs close together. "The obvious reason. I can't bear to be around him now. Given the fact that you've slept with every woman in the parish between the ages of eighteen and a hundred and eighteen, I'd think you would understand."

Beau annoyed her by calmly blowing into his coffee cup. "It hurts to know how little you think of me," he said, then a glint came into his eyes. "It's two parishes, by the way, not just this one."

Charly growled with frustration. "I'm glad you think this is funny. *I* need help."

After setting his cup aside, Beau grabbed her hands and held them the same way his eyes held hers. "Believe it or not, I am trying to help."

"You sure are going about it in a funny way."

Beau's expression grew wistful for an instant. "You aren't like me, Charly, at least not in this department. Maybe you haven't figured out why you slept with Marshall, but I have a pretty good idea."

"Lust?"

He smiled. "No washer and dryer for that answer."

She exhaled loudly. "Trust me, Beau, it was pure lust. I mean, the guy makes my knees go weak with just a smile. I should have known better. What?" she snapped at the sound of his laughter.

"I envy you, Charly. Truly I do." He stood and carried his cup to the sink.

"What is that supposed to mean?"

Pausing at the open door, he smiled sadly. "You figure it out. I'll give you a hint if you'll stop being mad at me."

Grudgingly, she nodded. "It has to be a *good* hint because I'm really frosted."

"I've never yet met a woman who could make my knees weak with just a smile."

"That's because there is no female equivalent for Avery," she grumbled a few minutes after he left.

"Is it safe to enter?" said a voice behind her.

"Speak of the devil," she returned smartly. "Better yet, *go* to the devil."

Avery was dressed in his workout clothes. So he was

going to act as if nothing had happened? Fine. She could play that game.

"I'm sorry you had to find out that way," he said, coming over to the table.

She refused to notice the tapered muscles of his thighs. Or the fact that he smelled of soap and spice. *Right, just like she could ignore a category five hurricane.*

"It doesn't matter how," she told him tightly. "What really matters is for me to know and appreciate that lying is as natural to you as breathing."

"It wasn't like that," he insisted. Apparently sensing her incredulity, he added, "Well, maybe in the very beginning."

She decided that lack of sleep was robbing her of any ability to maintain her anger. Suddenly she wanted nothing more than to turn back the clock. She wanted things to be the way they were before. Lord, she sounded like her mother.

"I'm tired, Avery. Can we save round two for later?"

"How about a fresh start?" he suggested. "No secrets this time."

She wanted to, but she knew that the pain of his deception would make that impossible. "I can't."

"Can't or won't?"

"Either. Both," she answered. "I really don't have the—"

She was glad when the ring of the telephone saved her from this uncomfortable discussion. Grabbing the receiver, she pressed it to her ear, then said, "Hello."

"Hey, Charly, it's Digger."

"Hi. What can I do for you?"

"It's what I can do for you. Are you interested in finding Jada's car?"

"Of course. Do you know where it is?"

"I heard the chief mentioning it to Johnson. A 1998 Mercedes was spotted at a hotel on Commerce Street in Baton Rouge."

"Thanks, Digger." She hung up the phone and reached for her purse. "I'm going up to Baton Rouge," she said without facing him. She related the information on Jada's car.

"Hold it," Avery said, standing to block her exit. "Where you go, I go."

"Don't be ridiculous," she seethed. "It's broad daylight and I'll be surrounded by people."

"Just like at the wedding?"

A shiver ran along her spine. "Nothing like the wedding."

His dark eyes narrowed, and his mouth was little more than a tight, determined line. "Since you aren't interested in being friends, I'll treat you like any other client."

"Good."

"Glad you feel that way," he said, taking hold of her arm. "I have some strict rules for you to follow."

"Rules?" she parroted.

"The first one is that you do whatever I say." He steered her toward the stairs. "It will only take me a minute to change."

"So change!" She gave her arm a futile jerk in an attempt to break his iron grip. "I'll wait."

He gave a derisive little laugh. "Rule number two

is that you aren't allowed out of my sight until I'm convinced you will respect rule number one.''

"I hate you.''

"That makes two of us, darlin'.''

CHAPTER TWELVE

"THERE'S A WHITE VOLVO in the far right lane that has been following us for the past ten miles," Charly said.

Avery grinned. "I'm impressed. That's Becca."

"Becca?" Charly reached out the open window and adjusted the side mirror to bring the car in focus.

"She works for me."

"Miss Pool Babe!"

He laughed. "If you value your life, you won't call her that to her face."

"Why is she following us?"

"I told her to."

"When?"

"I called before we left the house."

"Has she been around since the beginning?"

"Yep."

She regarded him for a moment as a litany of questions reeled in her brain. "So, how did my father find you?"

His grin was modest. "I've got a decent reputation in the field."

"How'd you get it?"

"I've never lost a client."

"I suppose that should make me feel better." She

pulled on her sunglasses and watched the trees lining the roadway blur into a green stripe.

She hugged her body, feeling suddenly chilled. "How long do you plan on staying?"

"Until I find the person or persons who want to hurt you."

"Then what?"

He reached out, capturing a lock of her hair. His fingers brushed her face in the process and it was all she could do to keep from giving in to her longings.

"That depends on you."

She wished they weren't in a car. "Meaning?"

"When I took this job, I never intended for things to go this way. It's never happened before. It's never been personal before."

She heard the sound of her defenses cracking. "You're confusing me."

"Good," he said forcefully. "'Cause you've got me so rattled I hardly remember my own name."

"You say the right things," she admitted. "Only I don't know whether to believe you, or if this is just a new ploy."

The muscles of his jaw twitched briefly. "Believe me. What will it take to convince you that I'm sincere?"

"Time."

Her answer apparently didn't please him. "Any idea how long I'll have to atone for your parents' sins?"

"This has nothing to do with my parents."

"Keep telling yourself that," he challenged. "I think this is worth fighting for, and I've never backed away from a fight in my life."

"Neither have I." She matched his conviction.

His smile was slow, deliberate. "Then, darlin', this ought to be fun."

"You'll have to save your fun for later," she said, pointing. "There's the exit to Commerce Street."

Avery steered the car off the highway and wove through several side streets until he hound the parking lot of the hotel. Charly picked out Jada's car and Avery parked nearby. Becca's Volvo pulled in next to them.

"Charly, this is Becca," Avery said as they stood together in the lot a few moments later.

The woman looked more like a pampered suburban housewife than some sort of clandestine operative, Charly thought. Her brown hair was pulled back in a casual ponytail and she was dressed in a tailored beige dress and tan flats. Charly guessed the woman would look equally at home on a tennis court or in a boardroom. She wasn't classically pretty, but she had an air of confidence and a warmth that was almost magnetic.

"Nice to finally meet you," she said. "Marshall has told me all about you."

"Wanna bet?" Charly muttered. Avery grasped her elbow in a warning gesture. "Nice to meet you, too."

Becca shrugged a backpack-style purse onto her shoulder and smoothed her hair. "What do you want me to do?"

Avery described Jada, then instructed Becca to go in and get her room number from the staff.

"They won't give it to her," Charly insisted, leaning against the warm car.

He looked down at her with a smug expression. "Becca has a certain charm. She'll get the information." His grin faded. "Stop looking at me like I'm a pig. There has never been—nor will there ever be—anything between Becca and me."

"I didn't say a word."

"You didn't have to. You have a whole vocabulary of eloquent looks."

She traced an imaginary circle with the toe of her sandal. "Is there some reason why the two of us didn't just go in and ask for her at the front desk?"

"Until we have some idea as to why she's holed up in this hotel, we err on the side of caution."

"Should I be scared?"

He cupped her cheek. "Not for your friend."

The innuendo kicked her libido into overdrive. The man had the uncanny ability to turn her into one big quivering nerve with a mere touch. She felt excitement and vulnerability in equal measures. But then...maybe the best defense was a strong offense.

Charly tentatively touched his stomach, silently pleased when she felt the muscle flutter beneath her fingertips. She met his gaze from behind the safety of her dark glasses. "Where is home?"

"I keep an apartment in D.C." His breath warmed her upturned face.

"But you don't spend much time there?"

"No."

"You and Becca run around the country like Nick and Nora Charles?"

The pad of his thumb made small circles against her skin. "Becca and I don't work together all the time, and I'm not *The Thin Man*."

Playfully, she jabbed at solid muscle. "Don't I know it."

He stepped closer so that his thighs brushed hers and desire rippled through her.

"Feeling reckless, Charly?"

She gave him a small push. "What an ego, Avery. Why would you think I was feeling anything? Anything at all?"

He gave her a mocking smile as his fingers burned a slow path to the side of her throat. "I guess your pulse is racing for the heck of it."

Flattening her palm in the center of his chest, she said, "People in glass houses…"

His hand fell away slowly. "Try being this brave when we aren't in the middle of a parking lot."

"I'm not stupid," she said, and ducked away. She hoped physical distance would calm her erratic heartbeat. "So, how did you end up going from town to town saving damsels in distress?"

"I did it for Uncle Sam, then I branched out on my own."

"What did you do for the government?"

Hooking his thumbs in his belt loops, Avery leaned against the Volvo, crossing his long legs at the ankles. "Mostly, I ran alongside limos with a microphone in my ear."

"One of those elite Secret Service guys, huh?" she asked, stifling a yawn.

"Am I keeping you up?"

She shook her head. "Sleep deprivation. I'm hanging on your every word." She smiled. "Promise."

"Why can't you sleep?"

She glanced down, concentrating on making a semi-circle out of small stones. ''I have nightmares. Some well-intentioned psychologist at the hospital said it was common for trauma victims to experience sleep disruption.''

''I take it you didn't put a whole lot of stock in her counseling.''

''I rank it right up there with voodoo and psychic phenomena. I respect those who believe, but it isn't for me.''

''Tell me about the nightmares.''

She scoffed. ''They're garden-variety nightmares. I'm sure they'll pass.''

''Maybe your subconscious mind is trying to communicate with your conscious mind.''

She laughed. ''Maybe there are death-rays on Mars. My nightmares don't make sense to me, Avery. Why do you think they'll make sense to you?''

''Try me.''

''Okay. I see Frank being shot. I see his eyes, then I see other eyes.''

''The shooter's?''

She shrugged uncertainly. ''I thought so at first, but then I see the eyes with no face.''

Avery held her shoulders. ''Do you recognize the eyes?''

''No.'' Her lids clamped shut as she concentrated on bringing the unpleasant image forward. ''I just see eyes and black and white.''

''You can't tell what color the eyes are?''

A piece fell into place. ''The black is above the eyes and the white is below.'' Slowly, she looked up at him, frustrated when her own brain refused to cooperate. "I told you it didn't make sense."

"It might."

"What?"

"Could you be seeing a man in a mask? Maybe he has a hat pulled over his forehead and—"

The face appeared before her with such frightening intensity that she reached out to Avery for support. Her mind's eye replayed the fraction of a second before she was shot. At first it was colorless and fuzzy, like looking at a negative. But slowly it came into focus. "He was in the woods," she whispered.

"Hold on to that," he urged. "Can you see his face?"

She shook her head. "I can see the red beam from the laser sight and his eyes, but he's too far away. He has a black cap—or something like that—pulled low on his forehead."

"What about the white?"

His question brought another flash of memory. This one was different. Where the other had been dark and colorless, this one was bright. So bright that she blinked to avoid the brilliant light. She smelled it then. The sterile stench of alcohol stung her nostrils, then evaporated.

"I can't move," she said as she felt her chest constrict. "I can't…"

"What can't you do, Charly?"

"I don't know" was her pained response. He pulled her against him, stroking her hair and praying that he hadn't pushed her too hard. He could just add this to the long and growing list of mistakes he had made where she was concerned.

He waited until he no longer felt the tremors rack her small frame. Forcing a smile to his lips, he said, "No wonder you don't sleep."

She looked up at him. Deep lines had appeared beside her pretty mouth. "What if the white light was a flashlight beam?"

"Could have been, I suppose."

A tear slid beneath the frame of her glasses. "Then Johnson and the others are right."

"Right about what?"

"If I saw him coming, I should have protected Frank. He didn't have to die."

"You just put the cart way out in front of the horse," he reasoned. "From what I saw of Johnson, he couldn't find his butt with both hands, so don't let him get to you."

"I just wish I could remember." She sighed heavily. "I wish it had never happened."

He draped one arm over her shoulder. "You'll remember."

"What if I don't? How am I going to go back to working with those guys if I don't know in my own mind that there wasn't anything I could have done differently?"

"Stop beating yourself up," he told her. "Those guys are cretins. Don't let 'em throw you."

"You make it sound so simple."

"It is simple," he said, leaning down to kiss the top of her head. "Wait until you've been on the job awhile, Charly. You'll—"

"Those are almost the exact words Frank said to me before he died."

"Frank sounded like a bright guy."

"He was."

He felt some of the tension leave her. Brushing the tear from her face, she tilted her head so that it rested in the crook of his arm. It felt good. Holding her made him feel complete.

"Frank was smart. He was one of those people who learned like a sponge. He spoke two other languages besides English and never formally studied either one."

"Sounds like a Renaissance man."

"Practical is more like it," she corrected him. "There are a lot of Cajuns in the area, so his French was a help. And he figured Spanish was necessary for dealing with the day laborers. It sure came in handy when I was with him."

"The traffic stops?"

She nodded. "I wouldn't have known what to do with those guys. Three of them were drunk, so that didn't help matters. But trying to follow the conversation with nothing more than one semester of high school Spanish would have been a challenge, anyway. Unless the guy asked me if the pen was on the table."

Marshall chuckled. "I never understood who decided it was helpful to teach phrases like 'The window is open,' and, 'My pants are green,' in language classes. Not that it makes much difference. We Americans are so arrogant we expect the rest of the world to master our language."

"Have you traveled much?"

"Ten years in the military, then some time with the foreign service before I became a member of the blue suit brigade."

Her laughter tugged at his heart. "You just described Agent Canfield."

"The cookie-cutter commando," he quipped, then caught sight of Becca stepping out of the building.

"Three-oh-nine," Becca sang out. "She isn't alone."

"Thanks." Marshall reached out to give his assistant's hand a tug. "Head on back to Riverwood and watch that access road."

"Oh, joy," she groaned. "Can't wait to bed down in my little camper by the bayou. Is Louisiana the Insect State?"

"You're just miffed 'cause you won't be able to see Charly's brother."

"Beau?" Charly asked.

Becca's sigh was long and telling. "Your brother has made this entire assignment worthwhile."

"Very professional," Marshall chided. "I'll be happy to introduce you when this is over."

Becca shook her head. "I'm just enjoying the view. Anyway, I'm outta here." With a wave, she climbed into her car.

"Do you keep logs or reports?" Charly asked him once they had stepped into the lobby.

"Yes. Why?"

She removed her sunglasses as they waited for the elevator. "I was just thinking they could come in handy. You know, a little incentive for my annoying brother."

"Blackmail," he grunted. "I'm sure you were a real pest of a little sister."

The small elevator compartment smelled of stale perfume, and the third floor wasn't much better. Cautiously, Marshall checked the hall, then held Charly to him as they stepped around the abandoned room service trays dotting the way.

"This isn't the usual place Jada picks for R and R," Charly whispered.

When he had located the room, he pressed his head to the door and listened. The faint sound of female voices was barely audible. Taking a piece of gum from his pocket, he tore off a piece, spit on it, then worked it with his fingers until it was malleable. He pressed it like putty to cover the peephole. After positioning Charly to one side, he knocked twice.

"Yes?"

He looked at Charly and mouthed, "Is that Jada's voice?" When she shook her head, he called "Maintenance!" through the door.

As soon as he heard the latch click, he reared back and put his full weight behind pushing the door open. A quick survey of the two frightened faces told him he might have overdone it a bit. But he'd had no idea who or what he would find inside.

Jada's blue eyes were wide with terror as she ran to comfort the younger woman who was sprawled on the carpet, thanks to him. "Who are you?" Jada demanded.

"The cavalry," Charly answered when she appeared at his side. "Nicely done, Avery. Later I'll try to find you a puppy to kick. I've been so worried,'' she said to Jade as she shoved past him into the room.

"Why?" Jada asked.

"Because we couldn't find you. Your father is going crazy."

Avery saw a flicker of remorse in the woman's eyes as she helped her companion to her feet. The second woman cowered, her red-rimmed eyes following him as if he had grown two heads. "Marshall Avery," he said with a reassuring smile, extending his hand.

"This is Tina," Jada prompted, keeping an arm around the other woman's trembling shoulders. "Tina, why don't you stay here and I'll take my friends down to the bar to talk."

"But—"

"I won't be gone long. Lock the door and I'll call up here before I come back. Okay?"

The skittish woman bobbed her head. She remained immobile when he uttered another apology before heading out with Jada and Charly.

"Who is Tina, and what are you doing here?" Charly demanded as soon as they were seated at a round table in the dimly lit lounge.

"I got a call from Peggy Simms, remember her?"

Charly nodded. "The prosecutor. What did she want after all these years? Please tell me there is some new law that will let them go after Mason."

"No such luck. But If I can convince Tina to press charges, Mason might finally learn the real meaning of the word *rape*."

Charly took a deep breath, then slowly let it out slowly. "What did he do to her? Jada, that girl doesn't look old enough to vote." She felt Avery's hand on hers, comforting.

"When did it happen?" he asked.

"New Year's Eve. Tina was a file clerk in Mason's office. There was a party…"

"Why did the prosecutor wait all this time to contact you?" he asked.

Jada toyed with the plastic ashtray at the center of the table. "I've known about it almost since it happened. But the prosecutor thought she could convince Tina to testify without my help. Tina is too scared. Because the records on my case are sealed, the D.A. asked me to try to get the girl to come forward."

"Does Mason know?"

Jada shrugged. "I'm sure. But I stopped giving that jerk the power to hurt me a long time ago."

"Why didn't you let anyone know where you were?" Charly asked.

Jada's eyes looked troubled. "Because I know the kind of pressure Mason and his associates put on me. I thought if I could spend some time with Tina before he got to her, it might help."

"How strong is the case?" Avery asked.

Jada's laugh was bitter. "Mason is slipping. There is documented medical evidence and photographs of her bruises."

"But?"

Shoving the ashtray in apparent disgust, Jada said, "Unfortunately, Tina's blood alcohol level was over the legal limit."

"He's going to get away with it again," Charly moaned.

"Right now I'm not so sure he believes that."

Avery held Jada's gaze. "Why?"

"He's a creep," Jada insisted. "But he's a creep who knows the law. I've seen him at least a dozen times in the past four months."

"Jada!" Charly cried. "Why didn't you tell me?"

"As if you didn't have enough going on in your own life? It's nothing I can't handle. Mason knows better than to actually cross the line. He doesn't have the backbone to do anything more than magically appear outside my health club or suddenly drive a hundred miles to shop in my corner grocery store. I didn't back down three years ago and he finally stopped harassing me. If I continue to ignore him, he'll find someone else to bother."

"Maybe he already has," Avery said, raw fury in his quiet voice.

CHAPTER THIRTEEN

"YOU CAN'T GO IN THERE!" the frantic secretary yelled as she made a futile attempt to follow him.

Marshall burst into the office, rattling the framed artwork hanging on the walls.

Mason Ranier clutched a microrecorder in his hand as he looked up with astonishment and arrogance in his brown eyes. "Who are you?"

"I'm sorry, Mr. Ranier," the secretary said. "I explained that you were—"

"I'm Marshall Avery," he interrupted tightly. Ignoring the flustered woman at his side, Marshall rested his fingers on the desktop and leaned toward the slimeball masquerading as a polished professional.

"Good for you," Ranier spat. "Alert security, Mrs. Kilmer. I don't see anyone without an appointment and *never* when they muscle past my secretary."

Marshall leaned closer. "No problem. I'd love to tell them all about Tina."

Ranier's Adam's apple bobbed above his neatly knotted silk tie. "Never mind, Mrs. Kilmer. It's fine."

Picking up a glass paperweight in the shape of an apple, Avery turned and lifted his hip onto the edge of the desk. He tossed the apple, caught it, tossed it, caught it again.

"That happens to be Austrian crystal," Ranier said.

"Then you'd better hope I don't drop it," Marshall replied with an insincere smile. "I'm not usually clumsy—only happens when I get mad. So you try not to make me mad, Ranier. I'll try not to break your little trinket."

"Is there a point to all this intimidation?" Ranier drawled in a terminally bored tone.

"I always have a point." Marshall tossed the paperweight higher.

"Would you get to it? I have a meeting in five minutes."

"We have a mutual friend. Several of them, actually."

"I find that hard to believe."

Marshall spared the weasel a glance, then intentionally bobbled the apple. "Has Agent Canfield been by recently?"

Ranier was out of the chair like a shot. His salon-tanned skin grew red as an angry flush seeped up over his collar. "I'll tell you exactly what I told Canfield—speak to my attorney. His name is—"

"I don't much care about his name. I'm not law enforcement," Marshall explained. "Which means I don't have to worry about all that Constitutional stuff. I'm a private citizen."

"Who can be charged with assault if you lay one hand on me!"

Rising, Marshall gripped the paperweight so tightly that he was afraid he would crush it with the force of his anger. "It would almost be worth it," he promised as their eyes locked. "Men like you make me sick. You don't even deserve to call yourself a man."

"Get out."

Marshall resumed his game of toss. "I have a few questions first."

Ranier's only response was to suggest a sex act that was physically impossible.

"No cursing," Marshall warned. "It makes me mad."

The man made a resigned gesture and fell back into his chair. "Hurry up and get this over with."

"Jada Crowley?"

"What about her?"

"Charly Delacroix?"

He watched as Ranier's face turned into an angry mass of red splotches. "She's a bitch."

Marshall lunged over the desk and grabbed fistfuls of Ranier's shirt, yanking him to his feet. "Wrong answer, scumbag. Try again."

Choking and sputtering, Ranier tried to catch his breath and talk all at once. "I haven't seen her for months."

"Know anybody who has?"

Ranier put up a useless struggle. "No!"

Marshall lifted the smaller man until his feet dangled like a doll's. "If you so much as *think* about Charly or any of her friends or family, I'll be back."

"You don't scare me."

Marshall tossed him back in the chair. "I should."

"JADA WAS RIGHT," Charly said as they sat on the back porch step later that night. "Mason doesn't have the guts *or* the brains to do anything as creative as trashing my apartment.''

"Sexual assault is about violence and power, Charly. Don't sell him short." Avery stretched, then slipped his arm around her shoulder, pulling her close. "Wanna neck?"

She breathed in the scent of his cologne. He was so solid where her cheek rested against his chest. "Smooth move, Avery. Learn it in high school?"

He tilted her face up to look at him and asked, "Did you?"

Charly giggled. "I went to a private, girls-only Catholic school."

"I heard you parochial school chicks were hot."

Giving him a little shove, she said, "Real hot. There's nothing like a bunch of gawky adolescents with hairy legs dressed in shapeless plaid jumpers and navy kneesocks to turn a man's head."

She felt laughter rumble through his chest. "God bless public schools."

"I'll bet you were the popular jock with the homecoming queen for a girlfriend."

"You'd be wrong. I was a geek."

"Liar," she huffed. "I'm right and you know it."

"Only partly. Tiffany was a homecoming princess."

"Tiffany?" Charly snickered. "Let me guess. She went by the nickname Tiffi—a leggy blonde with big hair and big boobs, right?"

He smiled down at her sheepishly. "How'd you guess?"

"The name," she said. "Somehow parents can look at an infant and determine her destiny with a name.

That's why there are no ugly Tiffis or Bambis or Bobbis. I think with a name like that, you're destined to dot your *i*'s with a smiley face or a heart. Avery!'' she squealed as he started to tickle her.

He gently fell back onto the porch, holding her so that when she fell, she landed on the cushion of his body. The playfulness quickly turned to something stronger when she felt the unmistakable evidence of his desire. A primitive need swelled from her very core, blinding her with fierce and potent desire.

Keep away from him. It will only get worse. Charly's hands were pinned against his chest, but it would require very little effort to push herself away. She should. Common sense told her that this was wrong. She reminded herself how easily and how consistently Avery had lied. He had only confessed because of misplaced guilt. She shouldn't risk giving herself to a man who could be gone tomorrow. But she was smart enough to recognize that Avery was special, unique. She also recognized that this man had awakened something primal and wonderful inside of her. The intensity of her own hunger both frightened and thrilled her.

She should push him away, but she didn't. Or rather she couldn't. Her rational side told her it was wrong. The woman in her knew it was right. She melted against him, groaning helplessly when he kissed her.

She felt him hard and urgent against her stomach. The mere thought that she might have such a strong effect on him came as a surprise. She raised her head scant inches and looked into his eyes. They were as black and as mysterious as a shadow. She felt powerful when he quietly searched her face, then smiled. And she felt something else. For the first time in her life, she felt beautiful.

When she dipped her head, she expected passion—greedy, desperate passion. So when he gently but firmly turned away, she was nearly overcome by surprise.

In one lithe movement, Avery had them up in the swing, side by side like two prim schoolchildren.

"Something I said?" She was relieved when the question came out the way she had intended, casual and confident. Two things she definitely was not feeling at the moment.

"No," he answered heavily. "I just have to learn that I can't touch you without wanting more."

Reaching up, she touched his cheek, turning him so their eyes locked. "I don't remember saying no."

He jerked away from her and pressed the heels of his hands to his temples. He stood. "That's because I'm the one saying it."

His words were like a bucket of ice water. She said nothing, wordlessly watching as he moved to the railing and looked out at the reflection from the pool lights.

"Is your objection to the act or to the partner?" she asked.

Breathing became a chore as she waited for his answer. His shoulders heaved several times before he turned around.

"I told you, I don't give critiques."

She held her hands up in a gesture of apology.

Ramming his fists in his pocket, he looked at her with eyes as turbulent as a storm-swept sea. "Do you trust me?"

"What does that have to do with anything?"

"*Do you trust me?*" he asked more forcefully.

Charly blinked. "I'm trying hard to accept what you did and why you did it."

"You danced around that one."

"What do you expect?" she cried softly. "It was a bit of a shock to find out that you're on Daddy's payroll. My first reaction was to put as much space between us as possible."

"You made that clear last night."

"I was angry," she argued. "The truth is, I don't know what I feel. But what's more important, I don't care."

"Come again?"

She smiled and went over to him. "I have two options. Either I can ignore you—" she slipped her hands around his waist "—or I can choose to enjoy this for as long as you're around."

She expected to find him smiling down at her. Her little confession should have put an end to any residual guilt that was causing him to hold back. It should have, but it didn't. Avery's face was like granite.

"You think it's that easy?"

She stepped back, her arms dangling at her sides. "Yes."

He shook his head. "I promise you, Charly, it isn't. At least not with us."

"How convenient for you to remember I'm a client now. A bit late, wouldn't you say?"

His eyes narrowed under her attack. "It won't work. I'm not going to let you avoid this conversation. You want to say nasty things, go ahead. But when you're finished, it's my turn.''

"That's just fine with me. You know why?"

"Why?"

"Because I have one thing I need to say."

"What?"

"I'm sorry."

After closing his eyes, he lowered his head, shook it gently, then gave her a half smile. "You are really something, Charly. I never know whether to kick you or kiss you."

"Gee, thanks." She felt herself relaxing. "I'd prefer not to be kicked. Can we do the kissing part?"

He made a sound dangerously close to a growl as he closed the distance between them. But then he stopped short when the door swung open.

Odelle glanced at them both disapprovingly. "Phone, Charly."

"Thanks." She kept telling herself she had nothing to feel guilty about, but it wasn't easy with Odelle giving her the evil eye.

"I forgot to tell you," the housekeeper said without any real remorse. "Mr. Jake called earlier. He said he had spoken to Chief Harrington and called the Slidell station when Miss Jada's car was found. He also said he got your message about Miss Jada and he was relieved."

"Do I need to call him back?"

Odelle held the door for her, then threatened to let it close on Avery. "Not unless you've come to your senses and you want Mr. Jake to come and toss this one out on his ear."

"Odelle!" Charly admonished.

The housekeeper tossed her shoulders back and pursed her lips. "Your daddy will have a fit when he finds out the two of you was rolling around on his porch like white trash. Hurry along now. Digger said it was important."

"Hey, Digger," she greeted once she picked up the phone. "What can I do for you?"

"Charly, this is Digger DuMonde."

Her smile faded and she grabbed Avery's arm. Why would Digger use his full name? "Yes?"

There was a moment's hesitation, then he said, "I think I found something."

Tilting the phone out, she signaled Avery to listen in on the call. "Found what?"

"Could you come and meet me?"

Avery got her attention and mouthed "No!"

"It's pretty late," she said.

"This is real important, Charly. I need you to come out to Swampy's."

Her heart missed a beat. "Why Swampy's?"

There was another hesitation, during which Avery became near frantic in his animated instruction that she decline. "I think I have something on the shooting. Can you meet me here?"

"It will take me a little while," she said, struggling with Avery for the receiver.

"Don't tell anyone, Charly. We'll figure this out, just the two of us, okay?"

The line went dead before she could respond.

"You are not going to some remote bar at one in the morning."

She matched the conviction in his tone. "I trust Digger completely."

"Then why did you look so worried?"

Scratching her head, Charly answered, "He used his full name, and I thought he sounded a little weird."

"Those are just two more reasons for you to stay put."

She touched his arm, imploring him with her eyes. "What if Digger really has something?"

Avery seemed unfazed. "He'll still have it tomorrow."

"What if he's in trouble?"

"He seemed like a big boy. He can take care of himself."

"C'mon, Avery. Digger is the only patrolman on the Slidell PD who I would meet. If that call had come from Johnson or Bill or any of the rest of them, I would just blow it off."

"You aren't going," he repeated, though she sensed a chink in his steely reserve.

"This could be my chance to finally know what happened that night," she pleaded.

"It could be a setup," he warned.

"Not Digger," she insisted. "He's believed in me since day one. He wouldn't ask me to do this unless he had a pretty compelling reason. I *have* to go."

"It's too dangerous."

A plan formulated in her brain. She started speaking even before all the parts had fallen into place. "You can follow me," she suggested.

"If you go, we go together."

Encouraged by her progress, she hurried on. "We can take your truck and you can hide someplace."

"That's what *you* should be doing."

She smiled then. "No. You specifically told my family that the best place for me to be was out in the open."

"I wasn't talking about this sort of situation."

"Please, Avery?"

"If we do this, I set the plan. Deal?"

"Deal," she agreed quickly.

"I'll call Becca and have her ready just in case there's trouble. Maybe you should call your station and see if any of your fellow officers knows anything about Digger being out at Swampy's."

Charly shook her head. "Didn't you hear Chief Harrington? He thought I lacked initiative at Jada's house. Do you know what he'll think of me if I make it two in a row?"

"He *should* think you're being prudent."

"We'll have Becca to back us up if necessary," she insisted. "Not that we'll need her. The only time Digger is dangerous is if you happen to be standing between him and a plate of barbecue."

"Still, I'll want Becca to meet us at the end of the drive. When do you want to leave?"

Getting on tiptoe, she brushed a kiss on his chin. "Two minutes."

True to her word, Charly was waiting impatiently by his truck when he emerged from the house two minutes and thirty seconds later.

"Sorry," he said, "Becca used this opportunity to

negotiate a bonus for being called out on such short notice.''

''I'll be happy to pay her—''

''It comes with the territory,'' he said. ''I'll drive until we get a few miles from the location.''

He started the engine and threw the truck in gear. Becca's white Volvo was a few hundred yards ahead, off on the shoulder.

''I can't believe it, Marshall,'' Becca said, walking over to the window of the truck. ''You finally found a woman who can live on as little sleep as you can.'' She stuck her head in the window. ''Hi, Charly. Maybe you'd like my job. I'll hang back in D.C., going to parties to schmooze potential clients, and you can go out on assignment with Iron Man. How do you get by on so little sleep?''

''Candy and caffeine,'' Marshall answered for her. ''She's on a perpetual sugar high.''

''Good system,'' Becca commented as she stepped back and reached into the Volvo to take out a radio. Marshall caught it on the fly. ''What are we doing?''

''Charly and I are going in first,'' he said, then gave directions to the bar. ''You'll hang back when we make the switch.''

''Why don't I go in as Charly?'' Becca asked.

''If everything is on the up and up, we could spook this guy.''

''Can you spook a man with a name like Digger?'' Becca joked as she got into her car. ''I'll listen for you on channel seven.''

''Don't tailgate me,'' he shot back.

A few minutes later, he headed down the deserted

road as Charly fidgeted in her seat beside him. "Ever consider going private?"

"What?"

He shrugged, telling himself that he was just making conversation to calm her nerves. He didn't mean anything by it. It wasn't as if he would jump at the chance to have Charly come work for him. If he did want that, it would mean he was thinking long-term, permanent.

"I like working when and for whom I choose," he said. "Ever consider it?"

"No."

"You get to travel."

"I love Bayou Beltane."

"You could work from here. In this day and age, if you've got electricity, you've got an office."

"I can't even get my fellow cops to respect me, how would I get clients?"

Working for me. "Just a thought," he said. "There are a lot of perks in this line of work. Perks you won't get as a city employee."

She laughed. "Like a Rolex and a closet full of designer labels?"

"I was thinking more along the lines of diversity, interesting cases."

"No offense, Avery, but I can't see myself crawling around in bushes taking pictures of rutting men for their wives to use in divorce court."

"I don't do that," he informed her, then relented sheepishly, adding, "anymore."

"Were those your wild days?"

The touch of amusement made her voice deep and sexier than hell. The possibility of them working together evaporated on that sobering observation. "What do you mean, were those my 'wild days'?"

Charly ignored his question. "Besides, I'll make a good cop," she said. "I just haven't had much of a chance to prove myself."

He wasn't sure if she was telling him or herself. "You are a good cop," he assured her.

Her fingers gripped his arm. It shouldn't have mattered. He shouldn't even have noticed such a small gesture. Normally he wouldn't, but there was nothing normal about his reactions when it came to Charly Delacroix. Around her, he found himself noticing the things he'd only read in hokey greeting cards. Like the way her hair reflected sunlight. Or the way her eyes captured her mood.

"Do you really think so?"

"Sure," he said after clearing his throat. "You're observant, Charly. That can be a better defense than your service revolver."

At her direction, he eased onto the shoulder, cutting the headlights. Becca pulled in behind them, doing the same. He did a radio check, then climbed into the flatbed and pulled the tarp around him.

"All set?" he heard Becca ask.

Charly got in the cab, opening the back window so they could keep in constant contact. Slowly she put the truck in gear and headed toward the bar. Marshall's powers of observation were second only to the power of listening to his gut. As soon as Charly said, "The bar's deserted, but I see his cruiser in the lot," Marshall's gut began to scream.

"What do you see?" he asked.

"He's just sitting there."

"Flash the high beams."

"Why?"

"Just do it!" he barked. "Well?"

"He's still sitting there."

"I don't like this."

The truck lurched as she rammed it into park. "I'll be right back."

"Stay here!" he called, but she was already half out of the truck. "Becca? I have a bad feeling."

"On my way." Her words crackled over the radio. "Avery!"

In response to the unusual pitch of Charly's voice, he tossed off the tarp and scrambled out of the truck. The sickly sweet odor told him what he would find.

Nothing smelled like death.

CHAPTER FOURTEEN

"DIGGER HASN'T BEEN DEAD long," Charly said. As much as she would have liked to turn away and bury herself against Avery's chest, she couldn't. "See that cassette tape?"

"Hard to miss, but I think that was the idea."

Charly started when Becca came careering into the lot. Her headlights captured the gruesome scene. "Want me to call it in?" she yelled.

"In a minute," he answered. "Bring me some gloves and tell me you have dubbing cables with you."

"The faithful and buxom assistant is always prepared," Becca quipped.

Charly swallowed, wondering how long it would be before she could joke in the presence of a dead body.

"Give me some room, darlin'," Avery said, snapping gloves over his hands.

Charly wasn't sure whether it was the sound of the gloves or the fact that she was standing in the same parking lot with another slain officer that brought it on. She just knew that the memory hit her hard.

"Faint if you feel the urge," Becca said. "It took me a whole year before I could look at one without losing my cookies."

"It isn't that," Charly said, gulping for air. "I—"

"She isn't looking too hot, Marshall."

When he came over and touched her, Charly gasped, her mind picturing a different pair of gloved hands. "He was at the hospital."

"The guy with the eyes?"

She nodded, concentrating hard to bring the memory out of the haze. "He did something to me. I couldn't stop him."

"What did he do?"

She tapped her head, as if half hoping that she could knock something free. "It's gone."

He gave her a wink. "It'll happen. Think Charly. You can sit in the truck if you want."

"No," she said, offering him a weak smile. "Digger died to get that tape to me. I want to hear it. What are you doing?"

Careful to disturb as little as possible, Avery reached in and slipped the tape recorder out of Digger's lifeless hand. "We're going to make our own copy before the cops arrive."

"Why?"

The machine opened with a loud click, revealing the tape in the process. "Insurance."

"I hope Digger was able to get whatever it was on tape before he died," Charly said.

"Me, too," Avery agreed.

Becca held a second machine that she had fitted with twin wires. Avery connected the machines together, closed the lid, then pressed play.

"Hello, Charly."

Her blood chilled as she recognized the voice of the caller who'd been harassing her for months.

"Officer DuMonde was a real fan of yours. Until I told him that we were working together. Until I told him it was your idea to kill him."

There was a short, vacant laugh, then the tape ended.

Just when she thought it couldn't get worse, she heard approaching sirens. "He's good," Avery said with disgust.

"What do I do?" Charly asked. "How am I going to explain that tape?"

After replacing the tape machine and tossing the gloves into Becca's waiting trunk, he held her cheek. "It will work out," he promised. "I can back you up on this. I heard the caller and I've been with you all night."

"Marshall will take care of you, Charly. Don't worry," Becca said.

But she *was* worried. Especially when almost the entire Slidell Police Department came roaring into the parking lot.

One by one the officers filed up to the car. They gave Digger the respect he deserved. They gave her the contempt she didn't.

As was proper procedure, she and Becca and Avery were separated. Becca was in the back of one patrol car, while Avery was standing on the other side of the road giving a statement to the chief. Charly was unlucky enough to find herself the detainee of Officer Johnson and his bad attitude.

He pranced all around her where she leaned against his cruiser, flexing his muscles and muttering remarks that didn't merit the dignity of a response. "You got a black cloud hanging over you, Delacroix?" More prancing and flexing. "Now you don't have *any* friends on the force. None of them lived long enough."

Pointedly, she looked past him, watching Avery hand his gun over to the chief.

"Poor Digger had it bad for you, Delacroix," Johnson sneered. "Did your boyfriend shoot him 'cause he was fool enough to want some?"

"Try thinking with your other head, Johnson. Maybe then you might be half the man Avery is."

His angry response was halted by the arrival of the chief. Not for the first time, Charly was glad to see her stern-faced boss. He handed the sack with Avery's gun to an evidence tech. "Let's have it, Officer."

She spent the next hour telling Chief Harrington everything that had led up to her discovery of Digger's body. She didn't include her nightmares—or details of her relationship with Avery.

"You'd better hear this." Johnson came up to them, breathless with excitement as he pulled the senior officer away.

Charly knew exactly what they were talking about. Silently, she counted. She made it to fifty-three before she was surrounded by officers. Harrington stepped forward, holding the tape recorder. It was now covered by fingerprint dust, but it still gave her the creeps.

"I think you'll want to hear this, Delacroix," he said without emotion. He pressed play and she was forced to listen to the voice again.

I think not, her brain screamed. She kept her head bowed, eyes downcast for fear that she might show some sign, some flicker of recognition.

When it ended, Johnson was the first to speak. "I'll take her in."

Harrington simply raised his hand. "Officer Delacroix and her companions are free to go."

Johnson looked as if he might blow a gasket. She smiled sweetly at him before she thanked Harrington and walked over to Becca and Avery.

Avery was the picture of propriety as they got into the truck—Becca in her car behind them—and waited for the police cars to be moved so they could leave.

Once they had gone about three miles, Avery pulled off to the side of the road. "Come here."

It was all the encouragement she needed. She scooted across the seat and buried her head against his shoulder. It wasn't only sadness at the loss of a friend that she was feeling. Digger's murder had forced her to face up to the truth. She was being hunted.

"You can cry."

"I don't want to."

"Do you need to?" he asked, turning her face up to his.

Charly thought for a minute. "No. I don't cry."

"You get mad," he said. His expression was grim. "Look, I know that you want to get this guy."

"*Will* get him."

"This isn't some backwater drunk using his wife for a punching bag."

Recoiling, she simply stared at him in shock.

He hung his head for a minute, and his fingers gripped the wheel until his knuckles turned white. "I'm not trashing your abilities, Charly. But this guy is a pro. It will take more than a good grade at the police academy and four nights on patrol to nab him.''

"I'm sure *you* have a plan. No doubt the great Marshall Avery can find him with one hand tied behind his back and his gun locked in the Slidell evidence room.''

Rocks and grass spewed out as he gunned the truck back onto the roadway. "I do have a plan. When you're finished playing angry female, I'll tell you about it.''

Finished? She hadn't even begun. He had dismissed her as a rank amateur. She had every right to be mad. In fact, mad was one of the things she did best. Hell's bells, growing up with her mother and father, she had elevated being mad to an art form!

"Are you going to pout now?"

The condescension in his tone burned her raw nerves like acid. "I'm just deciding what to say first.''

His hands left the wheel for a second as he gestured his frustration. "Why do I bother trying to talk to a woman who is completely incapable of having an adult conversation?''

"I can have an adult conversation. As soon I see an adult, I'll show you.''

"Very funny.''

"I wasn't trying to be funny. Your definition of adult means that I can't display a little temper. Fine. My definition doesn't include your this-is-a-man's-job, step-back-little-lady rationalization.''

"Great.''

"Great.''

"We understand each other.''

"Completely.''

"Fine."

"Fine."

Avery gallantly gave her the last word—and the silent treatment. By the time they were back home, she was more than willing to retreat to the sanctity of her room.

"Stay put."

The retort died on her lips. She was too tired to keep bickering with him. It didn't seem all that important anymore. And what made no sense was this heavy weight she felt whenever she and Avery were at odds. As a kid, she fought with Beau every second breath. But it had never left her feeling so physically drained.

She climbed the stairs as if her legs were made of stone. Her shoulder hurt, and she felt the beginnings of a headache. By the time they reached her bedroom, she was massaging her neck in a futile attempt to quell the dull ache.

"I'm too wiped for this," she told Avery when she realized that he was on her side of the closed door.

He came up behind her, swatted her hands aside, then started his own deep, wonderful massage.

"I'm sorry," she murmured. The feel of his strong hands worked like a tonic.

"Lie down."

She went on full alert. "I—"

"My motives are pure," he assured her. "Although I can assure you my thoughts won't be."

Charly fell across the bed on her stomach. She felt the mattress sag beneath his weight when he joined her to resume the massage. For several glorious minutes, she relaxed as his hands kneaded most of the tension from her muscles. How could one man make her feel so much? she wondered dreamily. His hands were capable of giving incredible pleasure.

Her mind took a predictable turn then. She was aware of the way his fingertips worked with a firm gentleness. There was a soft rustle of fabric whenever he moved. His deep, rhythmic breathing hypnotically urged her to roll over. It would be just that easy.

No it wouldn't. She recalled the scene on the porch. "Thanks," she said, wriggling out from under his hands.

Carefully wiping any expression from her face, Charly scooted to the edge of the bed, expecting him to leave. Instead, he flipped onto his back and rested his head against her pillow.

"Did I miss something?"

He opened one eye and flashed a grin. "Go to sleep, Charly."

"That was the idea. However, someone is sleeping in my bed."

He patted the pillow next to him. "Lie back. You won't even notice I'm here."

She glanced around just to make sure of her surroundings. "Avery?" She jiggled his pant leg. "You can't stay here."

"I'm not leaving you alone." When several moments went by and she still hadn't budged, he lifted his head. "Can't sleep?"

Not in the same bed with you. Rather than make this confession, she offered a mute shake of her head.

"How about if I hold you?"

That'll help!

"I'll talk until you fall asleep."

"I guess."

She crawled up until her head was on his chest. With one arm, he cradled her against him.

Oh, yeah, I'm thinking about sleep. She was afraid to move. Afraid she might rub her thigh against his, afraid she wouldn't.

"We should probably go to the hospital tomorrow."

"Today," she corrected him. "Why?"

"Maybe someone other than you saw the man with the eyes. I'm convinced your 'allergic' reaction to the medication was courtesy of him."

Each word he spoke sent a soothing vibration through his chest. In spite of herself, Charly felt her eyelids grow heavy. "I don't know what he looks like," she told him. "I still don't remember a face."

His lips brushed the top of her head. "Sleep, darlin'," he whispered. "We'll work it all out later."

SHE AWAKENED WITH A START. Brilliant sunlight streamed in the room. Sensing she wasn't alone, Charly turned and found Becca grinning back at her.

"Good morning."

She was confused. She was dressed. Avery was gone. Digger was dead.

"Marshall said you weren't at your best in the morning."

Charly regarded the other woman as she stumbled from the bed. "Coffee."

"Might want to consider something stronger," Becca teased. "Taking the hair dryer into a tub full of water will get your juices flowing."

After washing her face and getting that cotton feeling out of her mouth, she headed out the door. Becca stayed with her. It was like having a five-foot-nine-inch puppy. Becca had far too much energy and made far too much noise for this early in the morning.

Charly swallowed the groan that came to her lips when she found almost the entire Delacroix clan in the kitchen. "Don't you people have jobs?"

She walked over to the coffeepot but didn't miss the mild flirtation Beau offered as he relinquished his chair to a smiling Becca.

Her brother came toward her, choosing to sit on the countertop rather than drag his useless fanny into the other room for an extra chair. Charly agreed with his logic and hoisted her own fanny up, as well.

"Charly, we have chairs," Justin admonished.

"I'm closer to the coffee here. By the way, where's Avery?"

Shelby groaned and dug into her purse. She tossed a twenty-dollar bill on the table. "I'm paying under protest."

"A bet's a bet," Beau said. "Thanks, Charly, I knew I could count on you. Having a lawyer pay you is a great way to start the day."

"What are you two talking about?" Charly asked as her brother went over to claim his prize.

"Beau bet that you would ask about Marshall within ten minutes of getting out of bed," Shelby said with obvious censure.

"And you actually put money on it?" Charly asked.

"I know, I know," Shelby said. "You'd think I'd have learned by now not to bet with Beau."

Charly looked disgusted. "I hope you all stuck around here for something a tad more important than this."

"If my children would kindly stop acting like children," Justin stated in his courtroom voice, "we have pressing matters to discuss."

Charly shivered. The last time her father had used those words, he had gathered them together to announce the pending divorce.

Justin adjusted the lapels of his suit, and Charly braced herself for the worst. It was never a good sign when he donned his closing-argument posture.

"Marshall brought us all up to speed this morning," Justin said. "Some decisions have been made."

Here it comes! He's probably going to banish me to Siberia. "I'm not going anywhere."

Justin looked up, genuinely surprised. "You mis—"

"No, Daddy. I'm not going to run from this."

"Charlotte?" he tried.

"It won't work. The only place I would even consider going is back to my apartment."

"That isn't even an option," Justin said with a dismissive wave of his hand. "We decided—"

"Exactly who is *we?*"

"I accepted Marshall's counsel in this matter."

If his admission was supposed to make her feel better, it didn't. She would not sit by and let her father and Avery tell her how to deal with her own problem.

"Avery's counsel is hardly unbiased," she argued. Ignoring the look of utter disbelief on her father's face, she pressed on before she ran out of nerve. "I've only defied you one other time in my life. I didn't do that to hurt you or spite you. Law school was never for me, it was always for you, Daddy.''

"Uh, Charly?'' Beau half whispered.

"Hush, Beau,'' she muttered. Then, picking up her momentum, she continued. ''I'm sorry if this hurts you, but I have to stand and face this. If I don't, I'll end up looking over my shoulder for the rest of my life.''

"Charly?'' Beau said her name with more force.

"What is it?'' she snapped.

"That was Marshall's counsel.''

"What was?''

Beau tapped her forehead. ''Get your brain in gear so I only have to say this once. That great little speech you just gave was more or less exactly what Marshall said on your behalf not an hour ago.''

"He did?''

"He did,'' Justin verified. ''I have agreed to bow to his knowledge in this area with the understanding that his primary concern must be your safety.''

Her father kept speaking, but she tuned him out. What precipitated Avery's change of heart? she wondered.

"I think the bunch of you are crazy,'' Odelle scoffed.

"We have to respect their wishes,'' Justin countered. ''Marshall should be back in a few minutes.''

"Back from where?''

"He was wearing running shoes and a Walkman. You have three guesses,'' Beau teased.

The group began to break up. Shelby headed off to work, followed by Odelle, who was still fussing under her breath. Justin came over and kissed Charly on the forehead. She saw the anguish in his eyes and felt terrible knowing she was the cause.

"I'll be fine."

"I want Odelle to know where you can be reached at all times."

"Sure."

Justin hesitated briefly, then left without another word. Charly refilled her cup while Beau ogled Becca's long legs. "Don't you have work to do?" she asked him just as Avery came through the door.

"I'm working. Working on a broken heart."

Charly ignored Beau when she noted the deep lines etched into Avery's troubled face.

"Morning."

When he removed his headphones, Charly knew something wasn't right. His hair was completely dry and there were no perspiration marks on his shirt.

"You may not have to work, Beau," Becca purred, "but I do."

Her brother feigned a mortal wound to his chest. "I could keep you company. Hold you if you get scared, perhaps."

Avery looked at the two of them and let out a short laugh. "Forget it, Beau, my friend. She can crush a man with her thighs."

"It's Beau's ego that needs a little crushing," Charly observed.

Beau laughed and grabbed his briefcase, heading for the door. He stopped a moment and exchanged a silent communication with Avery. "She's all yours, pal. Good luck." Winking back at Charly, he added, "You'll need it."

"Be still my heart," Becca said with a sigh. "I could get used to that fine creature."

"You've got to hear this," Avery said as he took the cassette player over to his assistant. He passed Becca the headphones, then got around to giving Charly a smile.

"I hear it," Becca said, nodding. "What is it?"

"Background noise," Avery replied.

"So you weren't out running, you were listening to your pirated copy of the tape," Charly observed.

"Do you want to hear it?" he asked. When she nodded, he brought her the machine and placed the headset over her ears.

The voice wasn't as predominant, but it still gave her a shiver. Avery stayed with her as she listened. The noise he'd referred to was subtle, but definitely there. "Any ideas?"

He answered with an apologetic smile. Since she was seated on the counter, they were at eye level. Charly wanted so much to understand what had changed his thinking. Almost as much as she wanted a kiss.

"I think this would be a good time for me to leave," Becca said.

Yes!

"No!" Avery snapped. "I mean, I need you to take Charly to the hospital."

Disappointment filled her. "Why?"

He stroked her cheek. "I'm going to take this tape to Canfield. He has access to equipment that should be able to lift this sound off the tape."

"Won't Canfield know that you tampered with evidence?"

Avery shrugged. "I won't tell him if you don't."

"I need to talk to you," she said, pleading with her eyes.

He smiled as he touched his lips to hers. "We'll meet back here in a few hours. Can it wait?" He gave her hand a reassuring squeeze.

"Sure."

He didn't drop her hand. "You don't sound sure."

"I am," she insisted brightly. "This afternoon is great. I'm better in the afternoons, anyway."

"Lucas is arranging for Charly to view photo IDs at the hospital. He'll meet you there."

Becca saluted. "Yes, sir."

"Be safe," he whispered to Becca.

"You, too."

"Looks like it's just us girls," she drawled. "Know of any single doctors at this hospital? You could point out a couple or three of them for me."

Charly laughed. "I'm beginning to understand why you're attracted to Beau." She poured another cup of coffee. "I'll change and then we can go."

"Don't get too gussied up," Becca said. "I was kind of hoping we could take that cute little red car of yours."

"Sure," Charly agreed. "I'll have my cell phone then."

"Marshall won't let me drive anything that flashy. I'm supposed to be invisible when we're working."

Knowing that she was going to be at her brother-in-law's workplace, Charly selected jeans and a gray cotton blouse. She was just slipping on her shoes when she heard Avery's truck pull away.

"All set," she told Becca.

A few minutes later, her passenger had the stereo cranked up and the wind in her hair. It suited Becca.

"I have got to get one of these."

"I love it," Charly agreed.

"I'd love just about anything after that awful camper."

"The Volvo?" Charly asked.

Becca snorted. "I drive the Volvo, I sleep in the camper."

"Where?"

Becca held her hair out of her eyes. "I'm parked down by the swamp. No offense," she said, "but I don't know how you people stand it here. All those crawdaddys and do-daddys and only God knows what else crawls around here at night. I've been bitten in places where no man has boldly gone before."

"The swamp is a living thing."

"A noisy thing, too." Becca sighed. "Nope, I'll take the creatures on two legs any day."

Lucas greeted them at the entrance to Lakeview Community Hospital with a security guard in tow. Charly felt a little bit claustrophobic when Becca and the guard acted as human shields as she was led to a conference room.

No fewer than four huge file boxes were in the center of the table. "This will take all day," she groaned.

"I have to get back to work," Lucas told her. "Good luck." He gave his sister-in-law a quick kiss on the cheek and left her with Becca and the boxes of photographs.

Becca took her arm and pulled her to a seat. "Marshall will be busy for a while, so you've got nothing but time.''

"Meaning?" Charly grumbled as she accepted the first stack.

"Don't pull that on me. I know you and Marshall have something going.''

"Then you know more than I do.''

Becca patted her shoulder. "Count your blessings, Charly. Marshall is a good man.''

"I know.''

"You two got off to a shaky start, but that wasn't his doing.''

"I know.''

"He's in love with you.''

Charly's fingers stopped flipping through the index cards with photos attached. "That I don't know.''

"I do," Becca insisted. "In all our years together I have never known Marshall to be so careless.''

"Careless?''

Becca frowned. "You have that man so tied up in knots that he went off this morning without taking his gun.''

"Chief Harrington confiscated it.''

"There are others in the camper.''

Charly told herself that Becca was wrong. Avery wasn't in love with her. He hadn't taken a gun with him because he was going to the FBI. Becca was well-intentioned, but she was wrong.

Three cans of soda later, Charly still hadn't seen the face with eyes that haunted her sleep. "He isn't here.''

Becca shrugged. "It was worth a shot. Just because his photo's not here doesn't mean anything. There's still a strong likelihood that the shooter and the guy who screwed up your medication in the hospital are one and the same.''

Leaning back, Charly stretched her spine. ''My eyes are fried.''

''Speaking of fried, let's grab some lunch.''

She peered up at the woman. ''Do you and Avery have the same tastes?''

''He's all natural, no taste. Not me.''

''Good. Have you sampled our famous gumbo?''

Becca smiled, then her expression grew serious. ''We'll have to get takeout. You can't risk being too visible.''

''The hospital and a drive-through window,'' Charly grumbled as they left the conference room. ''Not a very exciting day.''

''That may be changing,'' Becca warned.

Following the other woman's line of vision, Charly saw Chief Harrington and Officer Johnson coming down the hall.

''Miss Delacroix?'' Harrington asked. ''I need you to come to the station.''

''Always happy to assist the police,'' Becca chimed. ''We'll follow you there.''

Harrington's expressionless eyes bored into Charly. ''This is an official request. I'm taking you in for questioning regarding the murder of Digger DuMonde.''

CHAPTER FIFTEEN

"A SOFT THUD AND METAL," Marshall said as he listened to the sounds for what felt like the zillionth time.

A lanky kid, who looked about fifteen, worked the controls of the sophisticated audio equipment like one of the great masters playing a concerto. "Could have been recorded near a chain-link fence. I think the thump is a footstep."

Marshall couldn't situate the sound. "What about an anchor? Or a flagpole?"

The kid shrugged. "I can't get it any better than this."

"Any luck?" Canfield asked as he came into the lab.

Marshall shook his head.

"While you and the nerd were down here, I took a chance and ran the voice through the computer."

"And?"

Canfield grinned. "Eighty-three percent match to one George Bernini."

Cautious optimism surged through Marshall. "Know anything about him?"

"The file should be coming through the fax machine as we speak."

As Marshall and Canfield worked through the maze

of offices like well-trained mice, Marshall felt a surge of optimism. He was getting close, he could feel it.

"Mr. Avery?" He stopped in response to the secretary's inquiry. "There's an urgent call for you on line three."

"You can take it in my office," Canfield suggested.

Marshall grabbed the phone and swallowed the lump of fear in his throat. "Avery."

"The police took Charly."

"Took?"

He could hear Becca's exasperated sigh. "'Took' as in didn't go willingly. As in being questioned in that Digger person's death. As in they even impounded her car!"

Leaning against the desk, he digested the news. He hated to think of Charly with all those bozo cops, but it might just be the safest place for her until he could track down Bernini. "Go to Slidell in case they have an attack of sanity and let her go."

"I'll have to rent a car."

"I don't care," he insisted. "Rent the Concorde if you think it might come in handy. I've got to go."

"I hope you're having more fun than I am."

"Something like that. Keep in touch. You should be able to get me in the truck."

He placed the phone on its cradle just as Canfield came in with a mess of curled pages. "Anything?"

The agent dumped them on the adjacent table and began to spread them out. He whistled as he plucked one page from the pile. "This is heavy stuff."

Marshall came around and read over the smaller man's shoulder. A string of expletives fell from his lips. "Bernini is wanted in seven different states. He's been implicated in at least a dozen contract killings. Who is this guy?"

"Freelancer," Canfield supplied tersely. "A graduate of the wiseguy school with a major in leg-breaking and murder."

"Wiseguy?" Marshall repeated. "Tesconti?"

Canfield shuffled through a few more pages. "Rico Tesconti and George Bernini worked together back in New York. They were close enough to share a cell for thirty days."

A flash of anger overwhelmed Marshall and he punched the chair. "It still doesn't make sense. If Tesconti is behind this, why didn't he kill us both the other night?"

"I'll do the paperwork for a wiretap. Maybe this time he'll incriminate himself."

"How long will that take?"

Canfield shrugged. "A day. Two at the most."

"Thanks," Marshall called as he bolted toward the door.

"Where are you going?" Canfield yelled. "You can't go looking for Tesconti, Marshall. You won't get within twenty miles of the guy."

"Watch me."

Marshall made record time reaching the Quarter in New Orleans. Leaving the truck double-parked, he went to the last bar he and Charly had been to before Tesconti's goons had jumped him.

The bartender's face had barely registered recognition when Marshall rounded the bar and grabbed the guy by the collar. "Where can I find Tesconti?"

Cowering, the man shook his head and raised his hands to protect his face. Marshall shoved him back against the counter. Drinks spilled, glasses broke and the few patrons eased back, giving him room. "Where?" he demanded as he pulled the man up by his hair.

"I don't know."

"Liar," Marshall spit. Pulling him up by his hair a second time, he said, "Last chance. *Where?*"

"An apartment above the pastry shop three blocks east of here."

Marshall went to the back room and yanked the phone line from the wall. He was given a wide berth as he moved toward the door.

"Tesconti will kill you!" the bartender shouted in a pathetic attempt to save face.

Marshall found the bakery and the backstairs to the apartment. An overdressed, muscle-bound thug was leaning against the railing with a cigarette dangling from his lips. Marshall went over to him and asked, "Got an extra one?"

"Get lost."

Marshall pretended to accept the insult, then whipped around and delivered a well-aimed blow to the back of the guy's head. "Rudeness will be punished," he whispered. Once he was sure the guy was out cold, he began feeling for a gun. When his hand came upon a hard bulge at the ankle, he took the weapon and headed up the stairs.

Through the window in the door, he could see four men in the kitchen, Tesconti among them. And there could be more in the next room. The odds weren't great, but he didn't have a choice.

Taking two deep breaths, he held the third and kicked in the door. "I can get off at least one shot," he warned, keeping the barrel trained on Tesconti's wide forehead. "Your flunkies can try to take me out afterward, but you'll already be dead, Tesconti."

To his credit, the man casually sat back as if he were presented with this option on a regular basis. "What do you want to know about before you die, Mr. Avery?"

"George Bernini."

Recognition flickered in the other man's eyes. "What is your interest?"

"I'm updating my Christmas list."

Tesconti's mouth twitched before he made a small gesture with his head. The goons backed out of the room, snarling and showing their still-holstered guns.

"I treated you with respect," Tesconti said. "You should show me the same courtesy."

"If Bernini gets to her while I'm standing here with you—"

"Her? The Delacroix woman?"

Marshall listened as Tesconti cursed in fluent Italian. "Do I need that kind of heat?" he asked Marshall. "Killing a Delacroix would be bad for business."

"You should have thought that through before now."

"Don't press me too far, Mr. Avery."

Purposefully, he applied just a little more pressure to the trigger. "I'm waiting."

Tesconti shook his head. "We live by a code."

"Show me in the codebook where it explains why you want Charly dead."

"It isn't me," Tesconti said. It was neither a defense nor an apology. "I told you, I only heard rumors."

"What were the rumors?"

"Ugly business," he answered, lifting a drink from the table. "In the old days we didn't involve ourselves in such things."

"Take a trip down memory lane some other time. For now, stick to the here and now."

"What do you know about agriculture?"

The man was playing a game, and if Marshall was going to help Charly, he had to go along. "Plant it, water it, harvest it."

Tesconti smiled. "Harvesting is big business these days. Huge conglomerates control the money, but it is still people who work the fields. Without them, the crops simply rot in the ground."

"Are the Delacroix doing something to impede the harvest?"

"You aren't listening, Mr. Avery."

"Charly did something? Or she saw something." Tesconti gave him a nod of approval. Marshall ran bits of her stories through his head.

We were the only ones who spoke English.

"The night before she was shot, she was in a bar full of migrant workers."

Tesconti sighed loudly. "Not the obvious, Mr. Avery. Life is about the subtleties."

"Her partner was killed. He spoke Spanish."

"So maybe this partner spoke to one of the people

in the bar. So maybe he heard something he shouldn't have.''

''What can a worker say? I'm sure Charly and her partner already know that migrant workers have a rough life.''

''Let me ask you something, Mr. Avery. What is worse than working for a pittance?''

He didn't hesitate. ''Working for nothing. They were illegals?''

''A real problem in this area, I am told.'' Tesconti took another drink. ''Lesser men than myself have been known to lure young men and women up from Mexico and Central America. These poor souls are forced to work for no pay. The conglomerates pretend they don't know what is happening so they can keep the price of tomatoes down.''

''What would make the price of tomatoes go up?''

Tesconti shrugged. ''The price would go up if they had to pay legal wages.''

''Who benefits by keeping the prices down?''

''Consumers,'' Tesconti said. ''Communities.''

''The community benefits from having a workforce of virtual slaves?''

''Some in the community.''

''Like who?''

''The farm owner, certainly.''

''That's the obvious answer. How about the subtle one?''

''There are some costs that are not reported to the government.''

''Transportation for the illegal workers?''

''And protection.''

Marshall felt his chest seize. "The Slidell Police Department is dirty?"

"Not the whole department."

"Who, then?"

"Sorry, Mr. Avery. I'll count to five now, and if you're still here after that, I'll instruct my men to kill you."

"FOR THE HUNDREDTH TIME," Charly said slowly, "I don't recognize the voice on that tape and I can't explain why he said we were working together."

Despite the stifling atmosphere of the windowless interrogation room, Chief Harrington hadn't even broken a sweat. He sat across from her, looking as stiff and starched as an altar boy at early Mass. Johnson was another story. His breath was foul, but it was still an improvement over his drugstore cologne.

"Marshall Avery can verify what I've told you," she insisted.

"Then tell me where to find him," Harrington implored without inflection.

Averting her eyes, she said, "I don't know *exactly* where he is at the moment." *Damn that tape!*

Harrington scraped his chair across the cracked tile floor as he stood. "Then we'll just have to keep you here until we can get confirmation from Mr. Avery."

"He confirmed it last night," she insisted.

"What else did you two do last night?" Johnson asked.

"That was uncalled for," Harrington said, and turned to look at Johnson for a change. "I think it would be best if we made accommodation arrangements for Miss Delacroix other than in the holding cell.''

Charly could have kissed him. The short time she had been placed inside that cage on the first floor was plenty long enough for her. The other prisoners were nicer than the officers. In the holding cell, she had been subjected to cruel taunts and crude suggestions from Slidell's finest.

"Like where?" Johnson asked. "She belongs in a cell with the rest of the scum.''

Harrington hoisted his utility belt and took a step toward his junior officer. Too bad the chief had ice water in his veins. She would have paid to see Johnson's Neanderthal features rearranged.

"I'll take her down to the file room. She can wait there until we can reach Mr. Avery.''

Charly was glad the chief was escorting her instead of Johnson or one of the others. She had a definite feeling that she might have suffered a fall down the stairs or some other "accident" and broken a few of her bones. At the least.

"Are you sure you don't know of a way to reach your friend?" Harrington asked. When she shook her head, he closed the door on her and locked it behind him.

The file room smelled of mildew, which was still preferable to Johnson's cologne.

"Come on, Avery," she whispered. "I know Becca has called you by now. What is taking you so long?''

She hoped he had come across some lead that would help. Frustrated, she yanked out the chair and sat down with her arms crossed. Boredom wasn't a very good companion. Then her eyes fell on the computer.

She turned on the switches for the central processing unit, monitor and modem, and waited for the machine to work up to power. She ran a directory for the system, then spent a few minutes hacking into the personnel files.

She typed her own name. The hard drive whirled as the information was transferred from the mainframe. The first few screens were nothing but the biographical information taken from her application. Next came the letters from her instructors at the academy.

"You snot," she whispered as she read a comment in one about her lack of self-discipline. Her finger wavered over the delete key. It would have been easy enough to alter the record. "Great Charly. Tamper with official police files," she chided. "Commit a felony while you wait." She smiled, thinking how much fun it would be to go in and alter Johnson's service record. She would never do it, but it sure was fun to imagine.

She scrolled down through the duty rosters for the days she had worked. Since her career was so brief, she would have to find some other way to amuse herself soon.

"Page one of fifteen?" she read aloud. "That can't be right."

Reading as she paged through the document, she tried to make sense of what she was seeing. "Someone screwed up," she muttered. The Slidell PD had given her credit for the five arrests Frank had handled. "December 10. Domingues, Felipe, nineteen. Probable

DUI. Possible INS alert. Suspect deceased December 11. No further action necessary.''

She remember Domingues well. He was a migrant worker they had stopped. Frank's grasp of the Spanish language had come in handy. ''Cars and alcohol don't mix, pal. Sorry you learned the hard way.''

The file also indicated that she had responded to the fatal accident the following day. She could guess how the mistake was made. Whoever was entering the information had simply failed to change the badge number to identify the officer. That explained why Frank's arrests were listed as hers.

''Clemente, Jose,'' she continued out loud. He was another probable drunken driver with a flag to remind the officer of record to check alien status with the Immigration and Naturalization Service. ''Jose, too?'' she mumbled, scanning down to the report on the fatal accident that had claimed the man's life the day after his arrest.

Very bad karma, as Marie would say. Except... ''I don't think karma strikes in threes,'' she said when she'd finished with the next record. ''Or fours.''

She knew what she would find before she got to the last arrest. The only thing different was the gender. Selma Garcia, sixteen, had also died after leaving the custody of the Slidell Police.

She heard the rattle of Harrington's utility belt and hurried to shut down the computer. With no more than a second to spare, she stood, more than ready to leave.

Harrington unlocked the door. He was followed by a large, burly state trooper with his hat pulled low on his forehead.

"Everything has been taken care of," Harrington told her. "I've arranged for you to be escorted back home."

Charly appreciated the gesture. "You spoke to Mr. Avery?"

"I got it all taken care of. No problem," Harrington said, leading her through the bowels of the building. "The red sports car is hers," he said to the trooper, and he pointed to where her car was parked.

That was nasty. Those jerks hadn't even had the decency to put her car in the lot. They had left it in the alley, between the trooper's car and a smelly Dumpster. "One scratch and I'll file a complaint, so help me."

"No one can help you now, Charly."

Cold fear made the simple act of turning around difficult. As she lifted her gaze, her knees buckled and her stomach lurched. It all came flooding back when she saw The Eyes.

CHAPTER SIXTEEN

"GOOD WORK FOLLOWING her car. I don't suppose you have a weapon?" Marshall asked as he crouched beside Becca in the pine forest.

"No."

"Since we can't share this one, you'll have to call for help while I get closer."

Becca grabbed his arm. "There's something wrong, Marshall. The trooper was driving her car and Chief Harrington followed in the cruiser. Who do I call, since the bad guys are all in uniform?"

"Jake Trahan. He's chief of police for Bayou Beltane and some relation to Charly. You find him."

"You be careful," Becca warned as he began his soundless approach.

Harrington was about ten yards ahead, standing next to the official vehicle. Marshall froze when the man looked around, then yanked on his utility belt. He heard the sound of metal handcuffs jingling. It was the same sound that he had listened to over and over a few hours earlier on the tape.

That meant the trooper probably wasn't a trooper, but Bernini. Marshall knew he was hidden by the foliage for all but the last seven or eight feet. He also knew that if he fired a shot, Bernini would hear it and kill Charly instantly. If only he could see Charly, but Bernini had parked farther ahead in the wooded area and Marshall could only glimpse the little red sports car.

He would only have one chance, and it had to count. Grabbing a heavy stone, he stood with his back against a tree trunk, his eyes fixed on Harrington.

Time lagged as he watched and waited. The stakes were high. One mistake and he could get her killed. *If she isn't dead already.*

Harrington looked up, giving Marshall the opportunity to lob the rock into the underbrush on the opposite side of the car. When Harrington turned to investigate, he jumped out and brought the side of his hand down on the back of the man's neck. There was a distinct crack before Harrington collapsed.

Marshall took to the woods again, careful to stay hidden.

He followed the muffled voices, praying he wouldn't give himself away as he traversed the dense underbrush. As he got closer to the bayou, he felt a rush of fear.

Bernini's voice was as clear and emotionless as it had been on the taunting tape he had left with Digger's body. Marshall was at least five yards away, but those five yards were completely open. He had to think.

That task was nearly impossible when he caught sight of Charly's profile. Her face was a blank mask, but he could sense her fear. Knowing her as he did, Marshall was almost certain that Charly would make a futile attempt for Bernini. He had to think! No, he had to act.

"You are really hard to kill, Charly."

"Or you're really bad at what you do," she taunted.

Bernini responded by giving her a shove closer to the swamp. As she stumbled near the fetid water, Marshall almost blew the whole thing by letting his emotions cloud his judgment.

"You can either see it coming or turn your back," Bernini said as he raised a gun on her. "Your choice."

"That's really accommodating of you, George," Marshall called out, emerging from the forest with a smile.

Whether Bernini was thrown by the sound of his name, or the fact that Marshall had shown up didn't really matter. He did exactly what Marshall had hoped. He stepped to the left and began waving the gun between the two of them.

"You seem flustered, George," Marshall commented. "I'll make this easy for you." He raised his hands. "I'll go stand with Charly so you won't have to look in two directions at once."

"I was going to leave you out of it," Bernini said. "But if you want to die with her, I'll oblige you."

Marshall eased his way toward Charly, keeping his eyes on Bernini. He needed to give her time.

"So, Charly, do you want to go first so he can watch you die?" Bernini asked. "Or should loverboy go first?"

By this time, Marshall had positioned himself in front of Charly. He prayed his plan wouldn't backfire.

"Neither," he heard her calm reply.

"You have to pick one," Bernini taunted.

"Then I pick you."

The single shot echoed, breaking the quiet calm of the swamp.

"YOU NEED A BATH and some sleep," Odelle said when Avery brought her into the house hours later.

"I need to talk to Daddy." She took Avery's hand and pressed it to her cheek. "I need to talk to you, too."

"I'm not going anywhere."

"This won't take long."

He flashed that sexy smile. "Take all the time you need."

Charly went into the study and found her father pacing. "You're safe." Justin strode over to her and hugged her tightly. "They threw us out when we came for you earlier. My God, Charly, I was so worried about you."

Charly patted his hand. "They *told* me a herd of Delacroix had stormed the precinct."

"A herd?" Justin laughed and led her over to the sofa, where they both sat down. "Are you absolutely certain that this nightmare is over for you?"

"Bernini was the man. I'm not sorry I took that gun out of Avery's waistband and shot him."

"Neither am I."

She shivered. "Harrington was using his position as chief of police to arrange to transport illegal workers up here. He used Swampy's bar as the location for some sort of sick auction." She took a deep breath before going on. "The night Frank and I went there to serve the warrant, he talked to one of the men. Frank wasn't involved. He innocently told Harrington that illegals were being smuggled through Slidell. And he got himself killed for it.''

"Marshall should have killed him.''

Charly took her father's hands. "Harrington won't get off easy. That much is certain.''

"How deep does the corruption go?''

"Nobody know's yet. The D.A. will have to try to find some of the illegals and hope one of them is willing to provide a name higher up than the chief of police. It will take months for this to be sorted out. Harrington was also pulling illegal aliens out of jail and turning them into the fields. He would doctor the arrest reports and show them as traffic fatalities.'' She gave her father's hands a squeeze. "I didn't come in here to rehash the gory details.''

"What can I do for you, Charly?'' Justin asked quietly.

"It's more like what *I* can do for you. I can apologize.''

"For what?''

"I've been punishing you for something you couldn't help. You didn't reject me when Mother left. I know that now.''

Justin nodded but looked terribly sad.

Charly wrung her hands nervously. Spelling her emotions out wasn't exactly her strong suit. "I've spent ten years acting like a child around you.''

"You are my child,'' Justin responded softly. "I have always tried to understand your feelings.''

Charly smiled up at him, briefly touching her fingers to his face. "I've been pretty rotten at times,'' she admitted. "But you *can* be a bit overbearing.''

Her father arched one brow. "I thought this was supposed to be an apology."

Charly nodded. "It is. I mean…I'm trying to make it one. I was at a really tough age when you and Mother split up. Bayou Beltane was all I'd ever known."

"We tried to do what was best for all of you."

Charly put a finger to his lips. "Let me say this, okay?"

Her father indicated he was willing to listen.

"I blamed Mother for leaving you, and I blamed you for letting her leave. At fifteen, I convinced myself that you could have stopped her from leaving."

"It isn't that easy, Charly. I wish it was."

She felt almost choked with emotion. "I mistook your strength for apathy. If Mother wanted to leave, there wasn't anything you could have done to stop her."

"You can't make someone love you," Justin agreed wistfully.

"I'm just sorry it's taken me so long to realize how much I've probably hurt you over the years. I hope you'll forgive me and we can move forward from here."

"I'm glad you finally understand, Charly. I hoped that one day you could learn to forgive me. I should be happy, but realizing what this means makes it rather bittersweet."

"It means I love you," she said, kissing his cheek.

"I think it means more than that. Am I right?"

"I'll have to get back to you," she answered. "Wish me luck."

"I don't think you need it."

Let's hope you're right, she thought as she climbed the stairs. She hesitated briefly before knocking on Marshall's door.

"Hi." He was wearing jeans and a smile.

"Can I come in?"

"That's probably a good idea."

Why did he have to be so calm and relaxed when she was a bundle of nerves? She remained standing at the door.

"You've made it this far, Charly. Don't quit now."

"I'm not a quitter," she said, fixing her eyes on the pattern of the wallpaper.

"Prove it."

He was laughing! She couldn't do this. "I *am* a quitter."

"No," he whispered, taking her by the hand and pulling her into the room. "You can do it." Once he had closed the door behind her, he gently lifted her and carried her over to the bed.

She found it hard to think straight when he was holding her against his bare chest. He sat down on the edge of the bed and Charly panicked. "I have to stand up," she told him, scurrying off his lap.

"I've never done it standing up, but—"

"Wait! You think I came here for sex, Avery?"

"The thought did cross my mind."

Taking in his sexy, tousled hair and half-naked body, she felt a flush warm her face. "Now I *know* I can't do this."

Avery was at the door and blocking her exit before she had even made the final decision to run. She looked up and felt her spirits fall when she saw the amusement dancing in his eyes.

"I have to go."

"Not until you say what you wanted to say."

"I can't."

"Sure you can. Try it one word at a time."

All or nothing. "Marshall—"

He kissed her with tender urgency and something else. Something new.

It took her a moment to realize that she was actually physically floating. He was spinning her around and showering her face with feathery kisses.

"I'm getting dizzy."

He set her down. "I love you, too."

"I haven't said it yet."

"Yes, you did," he told her. She was touched by the catch of emotion in his voice.

"When?"

"You said my name."

The full force of his words finally hit her. "You love me?"

"Only an idiot would walk in front of a loaded gun if he didn't."

Her heart felt as if it would burst in her chest. She'd never dreamed it was possible to feel so much for another human being. "You won't do that again," she warned.

"Swear."

"As your new partner, I will institute some policy changes."

One dark brow arched. "Partner?" His arms

wrapped around her waist as he moved her back toward the bed.

"Of course."

"No way."

"I won't work *for* you."

"I haven't offered you a job. And you have one—remember?"

She grimaced. "I sort of resigned when they told me they were appointing Johnson as the interim chief."

When they tumbled onto the bed, he kissed her deeply. Rolling over so that she was on top of him, he said, "There's only one way you can become a full-fledged partner."

"I'm already doing that."

He slapped her rear end. "No lewd inferences. This is serious."

"Can't serious wait?" She ran her hands along his torso.

"No."

She kissed the smooth planes of his chin and cheeks. "I don't feel like being serious."

"Anybody ever mention that you complain a lot?"

"Some guy whose name I can't remember," she said with a theatrical sigh.

"Will you remember it in the future if we're married?"

"Do we stay in Bayou Beltane?"

"Whenever possible."

"Do I get to be a partner?"

"After a brief training period."

She smiled. "Do I get a personal trainer?"

"Darlin', you get it all."

DELTA JUSTICE

continues with

FOR THE LOVE OF BEAU

by Margaret St. George

Dr. Holly Gibson had a professional dream, and a stubborn aversion to taking orders from men. Beau Delacroix, too, had a dream: he'd spend every waking hour working toward his goal to have a Delacroix horse win the Kentucky Derby. And until then, he had no intention of pursuing a serious, romantic relationship. And yet, from the moment the two met, Holly and Beau sensed a connection to each other the like of which they'd never experienced before.

Available in May

Here's a preview!

DELTA JUSTICE

FOR THE LOVE OF BEAU

BEAU ARRIVED AT the perimeter of the clearing in time to see Holly slither and glide through the dancers. Ducking low in the ferns on the marshy ground, he frowned and peered through concealing leaves, trying to figure out what in the hell she was doing. She looked strange. Her eyes were wide and sultry, fixed on a snake some man on the platform was wrestling while Flora screamed at him. Beau didn't give a damn about Flora's snake problems, but Holly worried him. A lot.

He'd never seen her move the way she was moving now. Her bones seemed to have turned liquid, she was that fluid. And watching her move was the most erotic thing he had ever witnessed. Although he wasn't sure if she was aware of what she was doing, she ran her hands over her hips and breasts as she might have done to entice and seduce a lover. The way she walked, the expression in her eyes and on her lips, the way she touched herself vibrated with raw sex. She was fully dressed, yet she created an illusion that she was naked.

Beau shook his head hard and tried to make sense out of what he was witnessing. He didn't know if he should interfere, although every instinct urged him to do so. Holly wore a peculiar expression and she moved in that slithery, erotic manner, but she didn't appear to be in danger.

Clenching his jaw and his fists, he swiftly searched the crowd until he found Desiree, standing away from the others beneath the feathery limbs of a tall cedar. Her gaze was riveted on Holly and her teeth were bared as if she were in pain. Instantly Beau understood that whatever was happening, it had moved beyond Desiree's wishes and control.

Something was badly wrong here.

No longer caring if anyone saw him, Beau stood up, fighting to figure out what he was seeing, not sure if he could believe his eyes.

When he could think, he saw Desiree staring at him across the hazy clearing, her gaze narrowed and intense. Her body was taut and trembling, her fists clenched against her chest.

"Help her now!" Her lips did not move, she didn't speak aloud. He couldn't have heard her if she had. The drums and rattles pounded at a frenzied level, building toward a crescendo. The dancers shouted and stamped their feet. Despite the chaos and noise, he heard Desiree's voice resonating deep in his mind. The shock of it paralyzed him for a second, then her words penetrated and all he could think about was that Holly was in danger.

Galvanized, he sprang out of the ferns and raced forward, feeling the heat of the bonfire on his face, throwing himself into the madness of drums and rattles, stamping feet and shouting voices. He flung someone out of his way and reached Holly as she swayed and dropped to her knees.

He was screaming, but he didn't know it as he gripped the snake's body and ripped it off her. He flung it toward the bonfire, scattering the dancers. Dropping to his knees, he caught Holly as she pitched forward. Frantic, he cradled her in his arms and pressed a hand to her chest to reassure himself that she was breathing. Then he stood and swept her limp body into his arms.

The sudden cessation of the drums was almost as shocking as the noise had been.

Shaking with fury, he stared up at Flora. "If you've harmed her," he said in a hoarse, guttural voice, "if she doesn't recover fully from whatever you did to her here—I'll do everything in my power to destroy you, so help me God! Leave us alone!"

HARLEQUIN  PRESENTS®

HARLEQUIN PRESENTS
men you won't be able to resist
falling in love with...

HARLEQUIN PRESENTS
women who have feelings
just like your own...

HARLEQUIN PRESENTS
powerful passion in
exotic international settings...

HARLEQUIN PRESENTS
intense, dramatic stories that will keep you
turning to the very last page...

HARLEQUIN PRESENTS
The world's bestselling romance series!

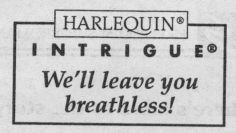

HARLEQUIN SUPERROMANCE®

...there's more to the story!

Superromance. A *big* satisfying read about unforgettable characters. Each month we offer *four* very different stories that range from family drama to adventure and mystery, from highly emotional stories to romantic comedies—and much more! Stories about people you'll believe in and care about. Stories too compelling to put down....

Our authors are among today's *best* romance writers. You'll find familiar names and talented newcomers. Many of them are award winners—and you'll see why!

If you want the biggest and best in romance fiction, you'll get it from Superromance!

Available wherever Harlequin books are sold.

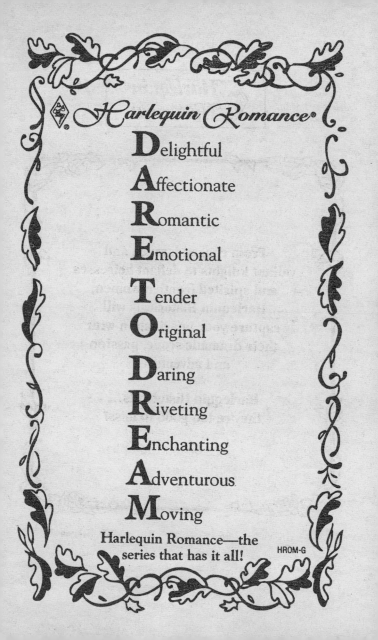

Harlequin Romance®

Delightful
Affectionate
Romantic
Emotional
Tender
Original
Daring
Riveting
Enchanting
Adventurous
Moving

Harlequin Romance—the
series that has it all!

HROM-G

Harlequin® Historical

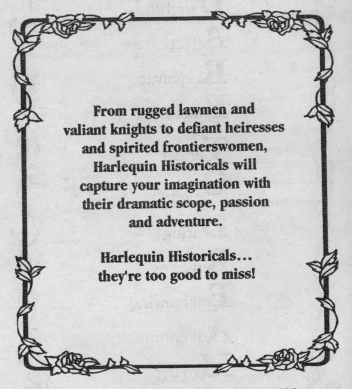

From rugged lawmen and
valiant knights to defiant heiresses
and spirited frontierswomen,
Harlequin Historicals will
capture your imagination with
their dramatic scope, passion
and adventure.

Harlequin Historicals...
they're too good to miss!

LOOK FOR OUR FOUR FABULOUS MEN!

Each month some of today's bestselling authors bring
four new fabulous men to Harlequin American Romance.
Whether they're rebel ranchers, millionaire power brokers
or sexy single dads, they're all gallant princes—and
they're all ready to sweep you into lighthearted fantasies
and contemporary fairy tales where anything is possible
and where all your dreams come true!

You don't even have to make a wish...
Harlequin American Romance will grant your every desire!

Look for Harlequin American Romance
wherever Harlequin books are sold!

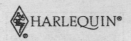 HARLEQUIN®

Not The Same Old Story!

 HARLEQUIN ◆ PRESENTS®

Exciting, glamorous romance stories that take readers around the world.

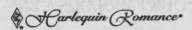 *Harlequin Romance®*

Sparkling, fresh and tender love stories that bring you pure romance.

 HARLEQUIN® *Temptation.*

Bold and adventurous— Temptation is strong women, bad boys, great sex!

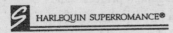 HARLEQUIN SUPERROMANCE®

Provocative and realistic stories that celebrate life and love.

 HARLEQUIN® AMERICAN ROMANCE®

Contemporary fairy tales—where anything is possible and where dreams come true.

HARLEQUIN® INTRIGUE®

Heart-stopping, suspenseful adventures that combine the best of romance and mystery.

 *LOVE & LAUGHTER*™

Humorous and romantic stories that capture the lighter side of love.